The Harm of Nature

Ella-Jane Jones

Published by Ella-Jane Jones, 2024.

THE HARM OF NATURE

First edition. January 7, 2024.

Copyright © 2024 Ella-Jane Jones.

ISBN: 979-8224084968

Written by Ella-Jane Jones.

For my Mum, the woman who has always supported me and everything I ever wanted to accomplish.

CHAPTER ONE

Crashing footsteps and fearful breaths cut through the eerie silence of the thickened forest as a young Brazilian boy and a middle-aged man bolt through the foliage. The man's light brown hair and sweat-stained, button-down shirt bounce frantically as he and the boy close in on their camp. Yet, as they continue to run, the sounds of numerous other boots gain momentum behind them.

Scared that these men are closing in on him, the boy checks over his shoulder, sure to keep his current speed. However, he has not escaped the view of the small army. They have weapons and wear matching body armor. With the fear of these men and their ability to capture them, the boy manages to speed up in distress.

Yet, this does not stop the angered men from drawing closer; however, the middle-aged man continues at his current and mediocre pace, allowing the child to pull away from their sights. After getting past them, the young boy slows enough to duck into one of the closer tent setups. It is where his mother awaits him and vaguely isolates them from the uncomfortable and dangerous events coming their way.

"They're here! We need to move you to a safe location! Davenport is here for you; we need to go!" Though the young Brazilian boy was quick to retreat from the impending actions, the man continued on his path with armed men following behind. However, the man inadvertently trips on thick roots running along the ground and slams into a jungle tree.

Agony momentarily rockets through his ribcage and palms. Although, he manages to get to his feet and allow his eyes to lock on a thin woman. A woman with long black hair, wearing a long golden and red free-flowing dress as she mediates on bare earth. The man steps into the naturally encased yet mystical circular space. Roots flow up and around what the woman uses as furniture, intertwining with a strange honey-tined pillar tucked away in the corner. It is a Thorne fit for a true Goddess.

The low dangling foliage allows for cascading shadows and deepens the effect. However, the breathtaking sight is the light piercing through the slight gaps between the various trees. The light dances on the soft dirt, swirling and swaying elegantly around the peaceful woman. However, despite the beauty of the space surrounding them, the stress of the events unfolding wears the man thin.

"We need to go."

There is a pause. It frightens Charles. He has been through enough with this woman to know something is wrong. She is vocal about anything that comes to mind to some degree. However, as she is silent, there can only be so many thoughts running through her mind now. She must have something almost ill-prepared but well thought of and potentially horrific.

"No, Charles." He is disappointed, knowing of the men sent after her. They are unempathetic and are only under Davenport's rule for the money. It means these men will point a gun at anything, especially the woman sitting before him.

While the woman is fine, Charles presses on, letting the ever-moving light dance on him as he attempts to show her how important the issue is. However, Charles is sadly disappointed as she sits with her eyes firmly shut. She remains focused on her meditation for now, revealing it has more importance to her than the army of men and, unfortunately, Charles.

A spark of fear forces Charles into a state of hyperventilation. Yet, through his troublesome moment of oxygen deficiency, Charles manages to calm himself enough to push the significance of Davenport's appearance. "How can— How can you say *no*? He's here to kill you. You don't think you should, I don't know, run?"

"To hide from him would give him the satisfaction of inducing fear," she begins. "Nonetheless, hiding would do nothing except halt natural movements and balance of the earth. And, if I remember correctly, it's precisely what Mr. Davenport is seeking."

Charles squats beside her, wanting and needing to comfort himself in this uncertainty. Her luminescent blue eyes open finally and focus on him. Yet, Charles does not need to express his distaste for the woman's decision as she notices Charles's distressed and almost empty persona. It is a sight she cannot ignore, not when she knows him so well and cares for him.

While still emanating her resting and calm state, the woman reveals signs of her empathy for him. She knows many of her followers are unprepared to face Mr. Davenport's raid like she is. Although, the woman is glad to have Charles by her side. He is the closest to the seat of power, and because of it, Charles knows the secrets and the Gods she encountered, the process of spiritual enlightenment, and the importance of the coming moments.

"What would you have me do?"

"*Go.* Go, help protect the children. You will be called upon soon, and you know what we need when the time comes. I'll deal with Mr. Davenport for now," she says.

The woman strides across her beautiful sanctuary, ending their conversation despite the numerous things left unsaid. Charles sighs as he does not want to leave her behind. However, he does what she asks and retreats for the children's sake.

As the woman continues to pace the small space set aside for her, a man decked out in full military gear enters. Though his weapon is on her, the woman does not panic. She does not appear to register it either. She only focuses on this man, as if she could read him. Yet, it does not take long for her to lose interest and turn away to look out to the thickened forest and what she knows awaits. "Beautiful, is it not?"

"Yes, it is."

"You're not Davenport. Tell me, where is he hiding himself? After all his efforts, I thought it would be him to confront me in this manner," she explains. "Yet, he has sent you. He sent you with weapons he knows will not affect me here. Not with my power."

The man pauses, unsure how to answer. Though, he manages to compose himself. However, this does not stop him from tightening his grip around his weapon in an act of insecurity. It is as though this would reassure him of his mission and his post. "He's on his way. I came to confirm your location and keep in contact until he arrives. It took him a while to find you."

"Yes, well, I imagine cutting down as much forestation as he did would help narrow it down. Wouldn't you say?" the woman asks rhetorically. "Yet, it still took him as long it did. He took too much away unnecessarily when I acted on necessities."

The man comes under slight distress, causing him to take steps back. Yet, despite the added distance between the two, his firearm remains set on the woman. Perhaps the man does this to show his strength, his courage against the overwhelming odds. However, they both are aware of the false sense of certainty. She steps toward him as if to put him at some ease. Yet, she appears to have failed as the man becomes uncomfortable with her oncoming presence. "What is your name?"

"It's Fredric. I don't— I don't know why I told you— I-I—," he reveals.

"Perhaps my charming personality appealed to you. Fredric. It's a strong name. Surely why you would have received it," the woman says. "It makes me wonder why you're here. A strong name for a strong man capable of making decisions and following his ideals."

"I'm following orders. There's no decision. What Mr. Davenport does for the government is his business," Fredric states.

The woman almost laughs. Although, it is clear that Fredric does not understand why or how his words are so humorous. Nonetheless, the woman regains her calm composure, returning her focus to the conversation.

"For the government? Is that right?" she asks. "Is that what you believe he is doing? You believe he is destroying all we know for the government. Oh, my dear child. What he's doing is to line his pockets. The very reason you're following these orders, yes? To fill yours."

Anger flashes across Fredric's face, his nostrils flare, shoulders become tight, and a rush of blood makes themselves known. The woman has pushed things too far. She must correct this before trying to go further. Fredric's stance on the situation could affect her plans. She must tread lightly.

She takes a soft breath and reigns in her current approach with him before her opportunity is lost. After a beat, the woman believes she may have found a way to get through to this man and save her potential good fortune with him and anyone he is with.

"I suppose I could be wrong. There could be another reason for following Davenport. His power, perhaps?"

Slight disappointment fills Fredric and the woman. She is wrong. Fredric does not seek Mr. Davenport's power. However, there is an element in his expression. It is something with an edge, something sad and concerned.

"No, I don't want his power," Fredric states. "Look, Davenport is here. To do anything but follow his lead would send me to prison. And that's if I'm lucky and nothing else happens. I don't know anything about him other than he's powerful, and I don't want to find out how powerful. I think anyone who does is a fool.

"I have a wife and daughter to consider. I'll put them before anything else. No speech, bribe, or threat will change that. So, whatever you're angling at, nothing can change my mind."

The woman pauses, realizing Fredric's commitment to his family and, to a certain extent, Davenport. Her eyes slant as she considers the best way to move forward, to bend Fredric's loyalties for better use. Though, she knows there is not much to influence. He is honorable.

"Fredric is a simple and kind man. I am glad to know Davenport cannot corrupt all following him. You will do your duties and continue to follow him. I assure you, I will maintain the things in this world that need be."

Fredric pauses before eventually nodding with slight hesitation. The weapon in his hands wavers and soon tips toward his feet, knowing he would not pull the trigger. Their eyes meet again, showing the understanding and respect they now have for one another.

Though, their brief moment of calamity is short-lived. A man in his later forties with long, slick-back blonde hair and a stark black outfit strides in from behind Fredric. A man who can bring them to an unnatural mix of hesitation and dread: Davenport. After immediately noting the woman's residence, Davenport slowly turns to Fredric.

Davenport's hand lifts and waves through the air, signaling for him to leave. "I relieve you of your stand. Go, join the others."

"You wish me to leave you with her?" Fredric asks.

Davenport's eyes drift, slowly focusing on Fredric. Mr. Davenport's seething fury burns into the poor man. It is enough to convince him to leave them behind. Still, he pauses, awaiting verbal confirmation. "Leave us."

Fredric does not hesitate and turns, hoping over various roots as he exits. Once Fredric is gone, Davenport's attention returns to the woman he had been searching for, to the woman he has finally cornered. Yet, to his surprise, he is not met with a rather vocal outburst or any physical violence he expected.

"Mr. Davenport."

"After all this time, knowing why I'm here, don't you think maybe *Mr. Davenport* is a little formal? Even for us? You could call me Scott," he offers.

As the words left his mouth, the disdain he sees tells him the woman would prefer to remain more than formal with him. Her glowing blue eyes dig into his distant ones, causing him discomfort despite his arrogant demeanor.

"I'll take that as a *no* then," he states. "This moment has been a long time coming, has it not?"

The woman smiles, keeping her eyes trained on Mr. Davenport's. His face remains frozen as he wonders what runs through this strange woman's mind. However, it does not get him far. He cannot predict in this matter other than what he has set into motion. Yet, he knows the woman intends to stop it. It worries him.

"For you or me?" Her words leave their mark on Davenport, almost sparking an instant debate between the two despite the ongoing conflict.

"Ah, yes. I do apologize. Forgive me for momentarily forgetting how God-like being's lives are somewhat eternal," he says with an excessively sarcastic voice.

Despite the chance to fire off the sharply worded quip he wants, the woman remains silent, letting her eyes rest on him. It digs at Mr. Davenport, denying him the chance to banter, to gloat over his accomplishment to capture her. Yet, they both know the silence will break in the coming moments. Whether it will be from the jackboots or the woman's eventual response is a question on her mind.

However, her curiosity soon gets the better of her. The thought of her capture leaves her to wonder what extent Mr. Davenport had gone through. This moment in time, while forced and somewhat anticlimactic for him, is almost everything Mr. Davenport has been working on most of his life.

"Tell me, how many men do you waiting for me back there?" she asks.

"A handful or so."

The woman smiles, angering Mr. Davenport further. Though, her smile is not from any form of delight. It comes from the lie on his part. He would not take any chances with her.

"I guess you would need them, wouldn't you?" she almost taunts.

The pair pause, waiting for the other to move. However, the woman grows bored and strides for the pillar set aside for her. Her calm movements anger him. He would have thought she would be attentive.

She sits on her makeshift honey-colored seat and gestures to an intertwining root system, signaling him to sit opposite. Davenport remains hesitant; however, he does what she suggests. Once he takes his seat, he lifts his attention to her eyes as if trying to look into her soul. He does this for a minute longer before finding something to ask.

"So, despite knowing what I intend to do with you, you keep calling me Mr. Davenport while I am yet to learn what I shall call you. I can't bring myself to call you by the name spoken by my father. Does this God have a name?"

"I did once. A long time ago. However, attachment to yourself is lost once you gain the honor of— Well, I think you know, now don't you, Mr. Davenport," she explains.

Frustration flushes behind his ears and reveals itself through his burning expression. Davenport does not appreciate the woman's vague answers and lack of confirmation. He is a man of order, living in a way he understands.

"It still doesn't give me an answer. What shall I call you?"

"The people coming into these quarters call me *Great Goddess*, although you do not seem like the type to call me by such a title. So, I ask you, Mr. Davenport, what would you permit yourself to address me by?"

Davenport remains silent as this had in some way gotten to him personally. However, to the mysterious woman's surprise, she is not met with a burst of rage as expected. She spots Davenport's facial expression softening. He is seriously considering what she had asked. After a moment, he returns his full attention to her with something etched on his mind and face.

"Well, what about Dame Nature? It seems fitting for— Well, Mother Nature," Davenport eventually concocts. "I would be honored to sit beside the Great, Dame Nature. It not only fits your title and ability, but it also reminds everyone that you are not a true Goddess. You were not born with powers. You were enlisted to bestow such overwhelming and commanding abilities."

"What do you intend to do with me again, Mr. Davenport?"

Mr. Davenport lets out a soft, half-hearted laugh. Though, he soon finds the humor of their situation to wear thin. His shoulders pull back again, and his eyes dim as if a saddening thought had suddenly crossed his mind. "Mmm, yeah," he sighs softly.

"You wish to kill me, cutting down all protected life that may stand in your way to do so. All to bend the natural way of the world, bend it to benefit you," Dame Nature begins. "It would shift natural remedies to suit the momentary need of man, not the earth. What is man without earth, Mr. Davenport? Have you ever thought to ask yourself this question? Because without the earth, man would be nothing. Man would either become extinct or colonize another planet. Do you know what man would become if we destroyed your home and moved on to another? A failure."

"How would mankind be a failure for preserving the earth?"

Mother Nature takes another look at who she believes is a sadistic and disappointing man. And for the first time, she finally realizes that Mr. Davenport does not comprehend the need for an overseer with absolute control. Perhaps she can explain it to him, tell him why she must take these actions.

"It would not be preservation; it would be an attempt at unnatural control over the earth and its habits all the while man continues to ravish its recourses. Slowly killing the planet and eventually, yourselves," Mother Nature tries.

"You speak of killing as though you haven't done a far bit yourself, great, Dame Nature. Do you forget the millions you've killed yourself? Floods, earthquakes, tornados, and whatever else you would think of. You've personally destroyed homes and families; how can you look down on what I wish to do for those people?"

"While I've killed people, Mr. Davenport, I've also given them fair warning to get to safety, but not all hear these warnings…. But the main difference between the two of us, Mr. Davenport, is while I do these things you speak of, it's for the balance of the entirety of the world. To kill a handful would be to save many more. It is the natural order of things and keeps the earth in its natural condition. Things are constantly needing a reset due to man's selfish impulses. Yet, all I do is a minor enhancement," she says lightly. "It shows how if it weren't for the constant disruption of men such as yourself, the world would be better off."

"Is that why you make these acts happen? To kill men like me?" Davenport presses.

Dame Nature pauses, knowing what Mr. Davenport is implying and trying to get her to admit. Despite the slight pressure Mr. Davenport is applying to the Great Goddess, she remains calm and non-wavering in the face of it. As if she could sense incoming persons, Dame Nature turns to where Mr. Davenport entered to find twelve armed men waiting for her.

"A handful or so?" she repeats for Davenport's benefit.

"We all knew it would come to this." Despite his words and the presence of numerous guns, the Great Goddess allows another smile to grace them. She thought something else would have come from this interaction.

"No, I expected you to use the gun you think you've hidden from me." The Great Goddess says.

She indicates the side arm underneath the back of his clothing. Mr. Davenport's eyes widen like a child caught drawing on the walls. As Mr. Davenport gradually recomposes himself, his hands reach to where he had hidden his weapon and slowly removes it.

"Yes, that's the one," Nature confirms.

"It was my father's," he announces. "I thought I might hold onto it while we brought you in."

Without another word, the burly men awaiting the Great Goddess step toward her. As a few of them place their hands around her biceps, Nature's fists ball from pain. Despite having the power of a God, extended life, and numerous followers, she was still valuable to mortal agony and death. Luckily, the magnitude that would cause her death is hard to come by. Unfortunately, Davenport's orders and personal attachment to this matter are irrelevant.

Nonetheless, Nature knows the events that will play out upon returning with these men. As they begin to exit her sacred space, they are amongst the ample setups of the Great Goddess's followers. They watch in horror and disappointment as she tumbles through their dedicated area. One of which is Charles.

His eyes lock onto hers as she is dragged through the treacherous landscape, revealing fear for her. Yet, to his surprise, she is not fearful. The appearance resting upon her suggests she has accepted her fate, although he is left thinking something else is present, something he hoped they could avoid.

"Charles, you know what you need to do."

"I don't—"

"You need to do it, Charles!" Nature calls while being pulled toward the distance. "Don't let us down!"

While Dame Nature and the men become separated from him, Charles notes Mr. Davenport's hovering presence. Not following the private army and the all-powerful woman he has been searching for, but momentarily standing, fixed on Charles. Almost as if considering what he plans to do with the man Mother Nature holds near and dear to herself.

However, he seems to discount whatever runs through his mind and turns to follow his men. Even through the long track back, his shoulders remain tight, thinking there may still be a chance Charles can do something. The sight of one of his best, Cameron Miller, a field tactician awaiting him, brings Davenport small solace and provokes a cautionary plan.

"Miller, I want you to keep a tab on that man. The one she was screaming to. I want to know who he is and what he does for the foreseeable future."

"Of course, sir."

In a final scan of the area behind him, Mr. Davenport faces a mix of relief and disappointment. With this, Davenport climbs aboard one of the jeeps alongside many of his armed savants before they pull away. Though, he visibly fights the internal battle raging inside.

CHAPTER TWO

It had been two weeks since Mr. Davenport had taken the Great Goddess, and Charles was no closer to completing his task than when he started. He feels nothing but pure inadequacy due to his current situation. With the Great Goddess away from her station, the world has erupted into chaos. Especially with the Earth's thinning atmosphere, ongoing global weather phenomena, and new space programs are launched almost daily.

Charles is one of the few who know the reasons behind the launches. It is to catapult a weather-manipulating software into orbit. Yet, while many devices have been on roughly the same trajectory, none have been able to manipulate the Earth as they had hoped. Not only was the intervention of the Great Goddess responsible for man's failed attempts at global dominance, but the very Earth itself and the natural course that it runs on soon caused the weather probes to become nothing more than the space junk they're surrounded by.

He knew that at a glance, many would consider control over the weather and the destruction it leaves in its wake to be a good thing. After all, he was one of them. However, he saw that these sacrifices were for greater reasons. Where there were no sacrifices, there was usually a parallel rise in the globe's overall carbon footprint. O2 levels would rise, and the number of natural resources would lower. If Mr. Davenport and those who endorse him continue with their current rate of progression, the planet will not survive much longer.

"Ah! Damn it!" Charles bellows.

Charles had accidentally slammed his toes into the stop sign before him. Though in pain, Charles strangely finds that he is more embarrassed by his moment of stupidity and clumsiness. Still disappointed, his eyes looked this sign up and down, wondering how he had collided with the pole. As the pain begins to subside, a familiar breeze brushes past his face, causing Charles to note the incoming storm heading his way. His attention shifts, searching for somewhere to shelter himself from the incoming destruction. Not that there are not many places for cover in New York.

However, his options have momentarily been limited due to the judgment that he faces with his current physical appearance. Charles didn't blame them for judging him on his newly thickened bread, tangled hair, torn button-down shirt, and dirt stains that covered him while proclaiming the end of the world and needing a new Mother Nature. If the roles reversed and someone else came to him with these crazy ideas, he wouldn't believe himself either.

Thinking he may have found somewhere to shelter himself, he sucks in a hopeful breath before stepping toward a fairly lower-class hotel. As his steps echo off the pavement, the distracted doorman turns and notices his presence. Charles stops between the set of double doors, looking inside at the almost empty interior, and focuses on the man in front of him.

"Would you mind if I come inside until the storm passes? I won't bother anybody," Charles asks.

Charles is hopeful, yet he does not expect anything due to his situation. Not many people will take him in. No one knows him or owes him anything. However, this does not change his predicament. Charles needs somewhere to sleep and stay out of the storm.

"I'm sorry, I can't. I'll lose my job if my manager sees you inside. I am sorry; I wish I could," the doorman apologizes.

"That's alright, I understand," Charles attempts.

Charles goes to walk away. However, the doorman's movement catches his eye. Charles looks at the man again, trying to figure out what he wants. Luckily, it is not to brush him away. The doorman looks at Charles with his mouth open. He has something else to say.

"But.... There is somewhere I know you'll be safe and warm. You'll even have food," he claims.

Charles's face sinks, believing he knows how the following conversation will unfold. He thinks the man before him will inadvertently shame him for his rugged appearance. Yet, Charles knows it may still benefit him. He does not want the embracement.

"Please don't tell me the soup kitchen or the homeless shelter," Charles pleads.

"No, everyone is heading there for the same reasons. But if you head three buildings down," the doorman begins, indicating to Charles's left. "There is an alleyway. If you go down to the end of it, you should find a metal door. Knock on it. They'll let you."

Charles is genuinely surprised by the amount of empathy that the doorman seems to show him. Especially given the reputation that New York has gotten over the years that Charles could confirm from his two-week stay. However, Charles is glad to see that there is a rare occasion despite the overwhelming sensation that he would be walking into a trap.

"Do I want to know what's behind there?" Charles asks.

"You'll love it," the man tries to assure.

Still suspecting the danger of knowingly entering an unknown space, Charles opens his mouth as if to question the doorman. However, the sudden cold rush sending shivers down his shirt pulls Charles's attention to the rapidly closing storm cloud. Being fortunate to know the Great Goddess for as long as he has, the sight of the cloud causes his hand to tremble.

"Three buildings and a metal door?" Charles questions.

"Yup, down there," the doorman confirms.

Charles's eyes linger in that direction before forcefully dragging his feet. However, Charles would have thought that he was walking against some secondary force. It is as strong tides hidden beneath the glittering surface, something hideous yet beautiful in the act of natural occurrences. As he eventually made the three-building stroll, the rain fell overhead.

The icy shivers that run down his spine. However, they are not only from the chilling droplets but from the dread of what lies behind this door. He wonders what the man could mean, what could be there that he would love, what and who could be lurking within. As the rainfall hardens, blurring his vision, Charles takes action and presses forward. Once reaching his destination, his balled fist lifts and sluggishly knocks on the grimy and rusted door before realizing that whoever is inside would not have heard this due to the excessive rainfall. He bangs again, although his knock has become sure and forceful.

"Hello?" Charles almost screams.

Though no one had answered, Charles widened the door. His hand hovers in the air as he allows his gaze to scan the area within. Despite everything within himself telling him to walk away, his curiosity and the chilling outdoors convince him to step inside. Although the space is relatively dim, Charles can still identify a slim, refurbished timber hall leading to a stark black, metal-grated staircase.

"Hello?" Charles calls again.

Charles closes the door behind him, and his feet slowly pace across the floor and to the staircase. As he gradually makes his way to the steps, he notes the few moving boxes yet to move from the awkward placing just off the accent. Charles soon stops at the bottom and stares at a warm, inviting glow waiting for him.

"Hello? Is anybody there? I hope you don't mind that I came in— I knocked; the rain, it was...." Charles trails off.

He begins to presume that he has walked into a backway to some fresh New York club or bar due to the faint vibration from the railing mixed with pop-punk music. Charles pauses for a moment. His heart almost sinks before he focuses on his reflection in the unevenly polished mirror hidden in the stack of moving boxes. The crazed look in his eyes, his messed hair, and untrimmed bread caused him to clench his fists. As Charles steps away from the stairs and heads back toward the exit, a young woman appears at the top and looks at him.

"Hello," she greets cheerfully.

Charles looks at the woman and needs a second take to note her features and question her likeness. In a haze, Charles takes a step forward to get a better look at the woman. He cannot help but stare. Yet, he tries to keep this in check.

"Hi," Charles squeaks.

He is unsure of how to proceed. Charles does not know this woman, and she does not know. However, he knows there is more to this meeting than him receiving shelter. It is fated and predetermined.

"Come on up. We'll get you dry and some food," the woman says.

This woman indicates for him to follow her. Yet, Charles stands unmoving, staring up after her, not knowing whether or not he should follow. Eventually deciding that it would be best, Charles slowly mounts the staircase and enters an almost empty and abandoned bar. However, the camping beds, electronic and fuel-based heaters, thermal blankets, a counter of food, and a few other men and women make the space seem more *lived in.*

"Come on," the woman says. "I'm glad you could make it in time; much rain?"

She gradually gestures to his drenched clothing and hair, momentarily pulling his attention to the water that continues to drip off him. Once returning and fixing his attention on the woman before him, Charles cannot help pausing as he only stares at her. As he continues to gaze upon her, Charles faces an uncomfortable familiarity that emanates from her, not only with her long, dark hair and the way she moves but how there is something odd and warming. It reminds Charles of someone close to him.

"I'm sorry, you are?" Charles asks, needing to know.

"Oh, sorry. I forgot my manners. I'm Sara. And you are?" Sara questions.

Her hazel eyes linger on him, patiently awaiting an answer. However, she is waiting a while. Charles cannot answer. He is stuck, staring at her. Charles cannot do anything else. She could be the one he has been searching for.

"Charles," he replies shortly.

"Well, it's nice to meet you, Charles," Sara says, handing him a towel. "We've got a full bathroom one floor up if you want to freshen yourself up before you eat."

"Do I look that bad?" Charles asks, knowing it is true.

Sara's eyes become wide in shock. She did not intend to offend or insult him, causing her a slight panic. Her hands shake as she tries to convey what she thinks. However, it does not stop them from knowing the truth.

"Oh, no! It's not what I meant at all," she defends.

"I was joking," Charles says, putting her at ease.

Charles smirks as he notices the relief on her face and how she releases the breath she is holding in. She did not think it was funny. However, Sara believes it is better to roll with what Charles was trying to do. She does not want him wandering the streets. It is too dangerous for anyone.

"Joking's fun," she says softly.

Sara turns away, letting him take another quick look around, finding that the space he stands within must be less abandoned than he thought. The floors are tidy, with no specs of dust on any surface and a small glimpse of a bedroom on the floor above. He had not noticed the spiral staircase tucked behind various camping gear before. From this angle, he can also see the somewhat quirky bathroom Sara had mentioned.

"What is this place exactly?" Charles asks curiously.

"Ah, technically mine, but it's under my father's attorney.... It was my Dad's before he died. He left it to me. I mostly use it as a place to crash," she begins. "I take in a few people here and there.... Especially now, the world. It's insane."

As Sara takes a breath, Charles notices her pride when speaking of the people she takes in. While many would assume this to be self-pride, the glance she gave to the people she brought in. It tells Charles that is not pride as he thought. It is the love she has for all she cares for.

"It's lovely. But, tell me, Sara, is it a good idea to take in random strangers and tell them that you live here?" Charles questions.

"Probably not, but I'm usually a good judge of character. Like how I bet I'm one of the few people you've met in the last few— I'll say days, but we both know it's more like weeks. You're not just some random homeless man," Sara alludes.

Charles remains frozen as he looks into Sara's eyes. He wonders what she could be thinking behind them and how she could have known anything about him. "What makes you say that?" Charles wonders.

"I know someone homeless when I see one, and they usually only look for somewhere to stay and eat and stay alive," Sara begins.

"That's what I've done," Charles almost defends.

"That's what you've done today. I've seen you; you're looking for something else, I don't know what, but you're looking for something," Sara explains, lifting several thermal blankets off a random, misplaced stool. "I hope you find whatever it is you're looking for. Whatever it is, it must be important."

"I might have, but I'm not sure yet," Charles says.

Sara looks at Charles, hearing traces of uncertainty and clarity. However, she does not question them. It is his business unless he chooses to tell her. Yet, it is not the only reason. Like Charles, Sara has priorities, and asking him what he has located is not one of them right now.

"Okay, that's great.... But, would mind— Just for a minute...." Sara says, signaling to the small crowd of people.

Charles realizes she intends to hand over the blanket and check on her guests, leaving him to step aside. Sara thanks him and graciously smiles on her way past, revealing to Charles that she is one of the few people he has ever met who still shows proper manners. While he is impressed by her genuine attitude, Charles finds himself more focused on how she tends to the people.

Many people would only do what they thought was enough or be polite because of social conventions. It surprises Charles how Sara checks in on her new roommates. Instead of only giving them what she thought would be enough for them, she goes to lengths to learn what they need and the familiarity she exhibits.

AFTER SHOWERING AND changing into a clean set of clothes Sara was kind enough to lend to him, Charles finds himself, again, staring at his reflection. He is free of the unnecessary grime, but Charles still faces his tangled, overgrown hair and thickened beard. His fists close tightly once more before picking up the razor Sara put aside for him. Charles's beard is the first to go. With each stroke, he finds himself again. He became free from the crazed animal many encountered.

Once Charles had finished with the overrun facial hair, he focused on the dangling parts of his hair. Without another thought, Charles took the end of the razor and nicked off the longest part before trying to even out the entirety of his head. While his appearance has imperfections, Charles becomes more at ease with his attributes. Charles swiftly cleans up after himself, not leaving a strand of hair behind. He then moves on, leaving the room.

As he steps out of the bathroom, Charles notes the dim lighting. However, what stands out to him is the silence masked by the storm. He looks over the railing to see many in their camping beds or cots he sensed the need to acknowledge. With this, Charles slowly lowers himself down the spiral staircase and into the same space. Upon reaching the sides of the people below, he can see through the dim lighting that there is not a single cot free for him to sleep.

"My luck for you," Charles puffs softly.

Charles scans the remaining space, searching for an area to rest. Once he realizes there is no space, Charles takes the nearest seat on a bar stool. While he would have wished for a bed to lie down on, Charles knew he would not have been able to sleep. His mind is too preoccupied and physically awake.

Various thoughts of the Great Goddess and her potential dynasts, not to mention the worry for those that face the backlash of Mr. Davenport's actions. While Charles and the Great Goddess knew that Mr. Davenport's attentions without the vengeful aspect were and are honorable. The idea is to save the majority of the population through weather tampering. However, some things should not be tampered with. The laws of nature included.

Yet, Charles doubts that Mr. Davenport has considered the ample amount of people he will inadvertently kill in the process. While the natural way to the planet they call home may not be perfect, it was fair. It was conditional, limited, and not bringing unnecessary destruction in an effort that eventually proved useless; everything has its purpose.

Shadowy movement captures his attention. He finds himself bracing for an attack as he turns toward the figure. It takes Charles a moment in the darkness to realize that the figure is Sara coming to his side. Relief flushes through his body before he wonders why she is here.

"You alright?" Sara asks.

Charles pauses as he looks over to the men and women sleeping before him, wanting to see if it would bother anybody to answer. As no one stirs, Charles turns to where Sara's voice had come from, where he knows she is waiting for an answer.

"I'm a bit cold, but otherwise, I'm fine," Charles admits.

"Well, then come over here, closer to the heater," Sara suggests.

Charles listens for a short second, searching for the source of the heater. After finding the faint hum, he slowly rises and sits by one of the gas-powered heaters. Charles lifts his hands and warms them before trying to locate Sara again. However, he cannot. Instead, Charles chooses to speak to the nothingness, knowing Sara will still answer.

"I'm not the kind of person that uses gas-powered anything anymore," Charles states strangely.

"Neither am I, but I didn't think it would be safe to set anything on fire. Fire safety is hard in a bar," Sara argues.

Despite the darkness, Sara knew she made Charles smile. She could almost always sense what people need, an ability she had developed as a child. However, this also usually came with a sense. She could feel their pain and other emotional conditions.

Many had labeled this as empathy. Sara always knew that it was somehow something more, something she was not always grateful for. It had brought her years of torment and isolation before she had learned to embrace it. Despite the downsides she still faces, Sara is glad she has learned to use her ability for those who need it. Yet, her empathetic-like abilities tell her that Charles needs some amity. One she has never come across before. However, what she can sense is that he needs her.

"I like your haircut," she begins on a softer note.

"You can see it?" Charles questions.

"I did when you came out of the bathroom. It seemed more you," Sara continues.

Charles's shoulders pull together while he becomes confused by Sara's comment. Though it was kind and something anyone might have stated, Charles does not think it is a random compliment. It cannot be.

"You don't know me. How can you say that?" Charles wonders.

Sara remains silent for a beat, considering how to answer and how to respond. As she and Charles sit in the darkness, Sara realizes that the answer to his question is what he needs her for. However, she does not know how to craft her response. It is difficult for her to answer him. She knows it will cement whatever he has plans.

"Because...... I think— I think I do know you," Sara tries. "You didn't want to look that way, did you?"

"No, I didn't," he states.

"Why are you here, Charles?" Sara continues to press.

"I needed a place to stay; I was told I would be safe here," Charles says, repeating his earlier banter.

Sara waits, knowing there is more. However, it does not appear that Charles will admit this himself. She must push him a little. Yet, Sara does not want either of them to deal with something they will regret. She thinks it will stop her from helping others like him in the future. Though, her fear does not stop her.

"I meant, what is it that you're looking for? What do you think you found," she clarifies.

Charles becomes defensive. He did not expect Sara to pick up on things he did not know how to deal with. It is like she can see through whatever keeps him from knowing himself. He never learned self-awareness in the same way as others.

"I don't see how that's your business," Charles almost blurts.

Despite the loudening of Charles's tone, the people in the space surrounding them remain fast asleep. Luckily, his voice was drowned out by the seemingly never-stopping storm that continues to ravish overhead. Sara gives Charles a moment, knowing that she has come on too strong. Once this moment passes and Sara notes her error, she tries to press him again with a softer tactic.

"You're right. I'm sorry," Sara apologizes. "I guess I— I don't know. I thought that you might know."

"Might know what?" Charles wonders.

"Might know why I feel like you need me," Sara explains.

Another thunderbolt passes somewhere off in the distance, allowing them to catch a glimpse of each other. Both were leaning toward each other as if revealing the sense of importance that came from behind what they had to say. While Sara had been rather forward with her point, demonstrating that she recognizes that Charles has some form of need to be near her, Charles remains a mystery. Despite Sara's ability to predict man's needs, nothing had truly prepared her for what Charles would expose her to.

"It's not just me that needs you," Charles states.

CHAPTER THREE

Although Charles's statement would have been clear enough for her to understand if they were discussing something simple, like social activities, Sara sits, unaware of the gravity behind what Charles had just admitted to her. Sara's attention remains fixed on where she knows Charles to be, waiting for clarification. However, Sara receives no further explanation.

"I'm sorry, but what does that mean," Sara asks, remaining hushed.

The silence continues to unsettle Sara. She leans forward in expectance or some other form of anticipation. Yet, she still is not met with any meaning behind Charles's statement. As Sara understandably becomes impatient, she hears the soft sound of what she assumes to be Charles's clothing. Her head lifts to find his barely visible silhouette.

"I don't think you'll understand...... Or you will, but won't be ready," Charles realizes.

"I don't...." Sara trails off.

With this, Charles makes his way to the stairs leading to the exit. Sara joins him in the cautious descent. They ensure that their steps remain silent for the sake of the sleeping guests. However, as they reach the bottom, Charles accidentally knocks into one of the inconveniently located boxes, causing it to topple to the floor. Charles and Sara pause, waiting to see if it woken someone above. Oddly, no sound follows, allowing Charles and Sara to proceed to the door.

"What are you doing?" Sara questions.

Charles's hand reaches for the handle and lightly grasps it. The cold from the touch of the cool steal runs up his hand as he waits for incoming lighting strikes. With a pause in the ravenous storm, Charles tries to open the door. However, he gets pulled back. Charles looks to his forearm. Sara is holding him. She appears worried.

"What are you doing?" Sara questions.

Charles considers his answer. However, it takes him longer than either of them would prefer. He knows what he is doing, but putting his thoughts into words for Sara is difficult. She will not understand unless she witnesses it.

"I have to.... I have to go...." Charles says, showing his exhaustion.

"Can't it wait until the storm passes? It's not safe out there. You could get hurt," Sara discourages.

"No. I need to go now," Charles presses.

As he turns toward the door, a sudden shiver runs down his spine, and his chest pings painfully. Charles's eyes cloud while he bows his head. He is thinking of the Great Goddess. Unfortunately, it is nothing positive or productive. It is almost a realization.

"Are you okay?" Sara asks.

She sees the agony resting on his shoulders. However, Sara does not get a verbal response. Instead, Charles allows the door to swing open. A gush of water almost immediately laps against his old, worn, and scuffed dress shoes, filling the hall with grime and litter. While Charles remains partially dazed, his attention drifts to the water. He soon looks at Sara, but her focus is on the entirety of the timber hallway in shock.

"Sorry," Charles whispers.

"It's okay.... Insurance will pay for the flood damage. I hope," Sara states.

Charles nods even though he is empty. As he steps out into the blinding downpour, a wave of responsibility washes over Sara, provoking her to step out after him. The combination of thrusting winds, water, and the brisk New York night instantly causes Sara to freeze. Although Sara is surprised, she reaches her arm out, searching for Charles. As if he had read her mind, his hand meets hers. While Sara had joined Charles for his protection, as their hands met, she knew Charles was in control. He gently pulls her along, navigating the seemingly endless dark blur. Sara tries many times to ask him where it is they're going. However, her voice disappears in the roaring sound of the storm.

"Charles! Charles! We need to go back!" Sara screams.

As he continues to drag her through what she assumes to be the streets, a bright flash of purple ignites the sky through the blinding mist. Sara and Charles stop abruptly, fixing their attention on the luminescent horizon. The color gradually fades, momentarily bringing them a sense of peace.

However, while the atmosphere slowly regulates and returns to its continuous haze, Sara notices the ground shaking uncontrollably. Luckily, it soon regains its stability. Despite the miniature quake, Charles slowly gains the confidence to lead Sara through the thickening water.

After a short while, Charles stops and finally releases his hold on Sara's hand, bringing her a great sense of uncertainty. However, he directs her to the soft Earth. Her gaze slowly faces the ground. While it remains dark and water continues to cascade around her, Sara can make out the thinning mud and blades of grass. She knew Charles had brought her to the park. However, the reasoning for doing so remains unanswered. Sara lifts her head to face him. She guesses that he is trying to tell her something. Unfortunately, she cannot understand him. Sara does her best to say this to him.

Once Charles realizes Sara cannot hear him, he closes his eyes, letting the rain wash over him. His head follows suit and lifts, facing the sky. Charles remains like this for a beat, soaking up the energy from the forever-coming rainfall. He concentrates on the pattern that the water relays and the strength of the incoming lighting strikes before reopening his eyes and focusing on where he knew Sara to be. Charles leans forward, pressing his lips to her ear. While Charles does not know if she will hear, he wants to try.

"Thirty-six," he states.

Sara pulls away, confused.

"What?!" she tries to ask.

Unsurprisingly, Charles does not answer. He had returned to his energy-gathering stature with his palms faced outward. Sara cannot do anything other than stare through the blurring rain at the man. Sara stands, battling the cold, knowing she needs to be there for him. Yet she still wishes she had stayed with the others back at the bar where it is dry and safe. As the seconds dully pass, her thoughts of the bar become more frequent. However, the sudden halt in sound and heavy downpour brings Sara back into reality. She looks about shocked before finding Charles staring directly at her.

"What was that?" Sara asks in a rush.

"Thirty-six seconds," Charles answers.

Sara stares at him in disbelief, not knowing how she should respond. Her mouth hangs open slightly as she finds something to say to Charles's expert prediction. Although, much of what comes to mind seems to be a miss for the significance of what he could anticipate. Once she realizes that she will not find words that would fit the situation, Sara decides that it is best to ask him directly.

"You knew when it was going to stop?" Sara questions reasonably.

"I was taught how to listen to the area around me...." Charles begins. "Does it say anything to you?"

"I don't— I don't understand," Sara says, dismissing Charles's hopes.

Charles stares deeply into her eyes, wondering how to reveal the world that he lives in and show her how to navigate and hear what the Earth needs. He releases a breath, noting how Sara is fighting the cold.

At this moment, something clicks for him. He slowly lowers himself to the ground and signals Sara to do the same. However, the sight of Charles sitting in *flood-level* waters seems to put her off.

"I don't know, Charles. I think we really should get back," she presses.

Sara's breaths are tight and restrained. She is uncomfortable. However, it is not Charles's fault. Something about what he is trying to tell her that worries Sara. She can sense the trouble and the pain it can inflict. Yet, Sara wants to know the world Charles is associated with.

"Please…. I promise you, it'll help," Charles almost pleads.

While Sara does not believe that whatever Charles offers will help her in any way, she assumes it will help Charles in another way. She feels his pain, worry, and something she cannot quite identify. However, it does not matter what else it may be. Sara has already decided to do this for Charles.

Sara lowers herself to sit beside him. Yet, it takes Sara a minute to steady herself against the pulling tide. Despite doing this for Charles, she still thinks this is ridiculous. Charles notices her reserved attitude and focuses on showing her how to do the following actions. Charles indicates for her to copy his gestures and placement.

Sara mirrors his crossed legs but forcefully relaxes her shoulders. She notes how Charles rests his hands on his knees with open palms and does the same. While she is trying to do this for his benefit, Sara's hands tremble, and her chest becomes numb in the icy air, causing Sara unbearable pain.

However, she pushes through her agony, hearing something within herself screaming the importance of this. Charles looks at Sara again, checking that she copies his placement, though they may be sunken in the ground. Her chest rapidly rises and falls in an attempt to keep herself warm. Yet, judging by her pale skin and blue lips, she seems to be failing.

"Close your eyes, take a deep breath.... Focus on the ground, air, and everything else that surrounds you," Charles commands.

Sara does her best to do as instructed. However, Sara cannot focus. She is too distracted by the icy water and the wind brushing past her. The chill is becoming too much for her to handle. It is all she can think about.

"I-I can't. I'm— I'm too cold," Sara explains.

Charles takes Sara's hands and gently places them in the water, allowing them to glide across the silky Earth. Though she continues to shiver, Sara can almost feel some form of power emanating from the soil. Although she senses the energy she now knows Charles must, Sara also detects a lot of agony and neglect.

"What is this?" Sara questions.

"What is what?" Charles asks.

Sara pauses. She is confused, and many thoughts run through her mind. However, she keeps coming back to the same question and realization. Sara closes her eyes and lightly presses her fingers on the ground. Her breathing slows, allowing her to connect with the Earth like she could with people.

"Why can I feel....? Feel the Earth?" Sara perplexes. "I didn't know...."

Charles smiles, knowing that he has done something right. However, he composes himself, understanding what Sara is going through. His only issue now is getting Sara to comprehend what she is experiencing.

"You know, empathy is felt for all living things.... The globe included. You just never knew that you could communicate with it before. You never knew that you could sense what it requires, anticipate set movements," Charles explains. "It took me a long time to be fully aware of my surroundings, years of training. But the few people like you, it comes to them— To you naturally."

Sara takes a long moment to connect with the space that encircles her, trying to solve what is causing the escalating damage that it has undergone in such a short time. The agony that the Earth seems to be going through appears to be recent as if something had only recently taken place. After a moment, Sara assumed the glowing skies and tremendous, unnatural earthquake to be the cause or some side effect.

"The pain isn't anything I think I've ever felt before," Sara says.

Sara turns her attention to Charles, hoping he will know what she means. As she hoped, Charles knows what she is referring to. Unfortunately, it is not what anyone wants. It will result in much more agony and torture.

"It's mourning," Charles proclaims.

"Mourning what?" Sara questions.

Charles turns away, searching for something out in the space before him. The expression behind his eyes instantly triggers Sara's bewilderment and her fears. While Sara stews on her newly found phobias, Charles finally returns his full attention to her.

"You sure you're ready?" Charles asks. "Once I tell you, there will be no turning back."

It takes Sara a minute to consider refusing to acknowledge what Charles wants to say. However, she finds that her curiosity soon gets the better of her. She must know what is happening and why it is happening.

"I want to know what it could be mourning. I didn't know a planet could mourn," Sara presses

"Our planet can do lots of things. Mourn, fight, and reset to its natural and primal state. And when it's needed, help heal those in need," Charles alludes.

While Sara could understand most of what Charles has said, she continues to wonder what a planet could mourn over. Although she has not obtained an answer surrounding the planet's somewhat emotional quarrel, Sara finds herself stuck on something else Charles had said. She could not completely agree with all his points as there seemed to be a particular flaw.

"A planet can't help heal the people. The people have to heal themselves from things from the planet," Sara argues. "It takes time to develop cures and other modern medicines. The people had to figure it out."

Charles chuckles, knowing the skepticism holding her captive all too well. He eventually allows his chest to fall as he releases a breath Charles was unaware he was holding. His mind drifts, trying to find a way to show that what Charles revealed was true. He turns his attention to their positioning in the mud and flood water, realizing that the answer is closer to him than he thought.

"You know, several generations of monks could prove you wrong. Have you ever studied beside them? Watched how they can achieve what many would call superhuman feats?" Charles questions to prove his point.

"No," Sara says. "I can't say that I have…. But I don't see how that has anything to do with what you're saying."

Charles gives a soft and genuine smile.

"How do you feel?" he asks.

Sara pauses, confused. There seems to be nothing worth fusing over. She is happy, calm, and warm. As these thoughts finally come to mind, Sara's eyes widen, realizing what Charles was asking her.

"How….? How….?" Sara tires.

"Like the monks, connecting with nature, becoming one with your surroundings allowed the Earth to heal you…. In this case, regulate and raise your body temperature," Charles explains. "Do you still think these things are impossible?"

She focuses on the space before her, pondering the idea that the Earth could be capable of such miraculous feats. As she begins to accept that Charles has shown her that these things are indeed possible and that she has access to them, the expression written on Charles's face saddens her. Sara soon picks up on Charles's woes and trains her full attention on him.

"What is it?" she asks.

Charles considers how to answer Sara. While the answers were clear, he does not think he should bring up the full extent of his worries. As he knows she continues to look at him patiently, Charles turns, noticing the raw emotion in her eyes.

"You remind me of someone I knew once," Charles dismisses.

"Is that good or bad?" Sara questions.

Charles chuckles despite knowing that Sara is serious. It is not from finding anything humorous. It is his weariness that wears him down.

"It's a good thing. Especially moving forward," Charles says.

Charles stands and slowly heads back toward the bar. Sara follows. However, her lip twitches as she tries to get a straight answer from him. She must know and will not stop until she gets the answers.

"What does that mean?" Sara presses.

His pace slows, allowing her to catch up, not that he could judge her for struggling against the strong tide of the water. Charles finds it difficult to press through it as well. As they near the long iron fence stretching across the park, Charles stops and gently holds on to it like a railing. Sara stops beside him, still awaiting his response.

"What do you think about the Amazon?" Charles asks strangely.

Sara knows there is something more significant behind his question. However, she does not know what it is. She needs him to enlighten her. Unfortunately, it does not look like he will tell her yet. Sara must give him a little push.

"The Amazon? I-I think it's beautiful.... But I think it would be unbearable in the summer," Sara states.

The grimace on Charles's face momentarily slips away and becomes replaced with a smirk. Sara stews with the thought of the Amazon, wondering why Charles could think this was an important topic to discuss when he had just shown her something miraculous. As Sara imagines him insinuating that those feats and the Amazon connect by means she cannot fully understand, Charles's focus shifts upward.

Sara follows his line of sight to see the storm cloud slowly drifting off toward the distance before noting the numerous and visible chain of satellites. Their attention stays there, thinking to themselves. However, while Charles goes through the same pitch he must sell her on, Sara debates with herself.

"What do you think of those?" Charles asks.

His mind is still off in the distance. However, Sara returns to reality and stares at Charles, waiting for him to join her. Unfortunately, it takes longer than she imagined, and Charles does not fully return. He is almost like a shadow to himself, stuck thinking of something else. Yet, Sara knows he still wants an answer.

"I think the idea behind them is noble.... But I have a feeling that there's something wrong with it, something that we shouldn't test," Sara says truthfully.

Charles nods, finally believing with his whole heart and mind that he has indeed done right by the Great Goddess. He thinks he has a chance at fighting for world order. Yet, the only thing that might change this is Sara's thoughts and beliefs.

"Oh, Sara. One last thing," Charles begins. "What do you think about Washington this time of year?"

CHAPTER FOUR

Sara thought all fights remained grounded until further notice. However, she was wrong. The storm over New York settled once she accepted the truth. It was the same with Washington. Charles muttered something about it, and Sara. Unfortunately, Sara missed whatever he was trying to say. It did not make any sense to her.

It was her first airplane ride. She was nervous. However, it appears like she had a fair reason. The flight into Washington was a terrifying experience. With the constant weather-related anomalies, Sara and many fellow passengers were uncomfortable on board. Luckily for her, the flight was nearing its end. She turns, finding Charles still fast asleep. Not that she could call it sleep; he is unconscious. Charles had known before the flight that it would be difficult. It naturally led to his cocktail of sleeping pills.

Sara decided to skip the sleep-inducing pills, thinking they were dangerous. However, she did not judge him for wanting to remain in a consistent blackout through the flight from hell. Knowing that they are nearing Washington, Sara realizes she must correct Charles's seat before they come in for the landing. She awkwardly does so before checking his seatbelt.

"There we go," she whispers, satisfied.

As the seatbelt fastening sign lights up, the flight attendant walks by, checking that Charles is secure. With a nod from both the woman and Sara, the flight attendant continues on her way. Through the window, Sara can see the runway in the distance. However, the blissful sight of the tarmac is interrupted by the intermediate turbulence that forces Sara's grip on her armrest to tighten. The tips of her fingers have naturally gone white, and her heart rate has risen beyond what she believes to be safe. Thankfully, rumbling through the entirety of the plane eventually begins to fade, granting her the ability to breathe.

"Captain Marcel here. Once again, I'm sorry for the turbulence that we've been experiencing. But in better news, we are about to make out decent. Please make sure that all your seatbelts are fastened and sit tight, knowing that we'll be safely on the ground in no time," the captain attempts to reassure.

As Sara and her fellow passengers mentally prepare themselves for landing, she catches movement from the corner of her eye. Initially thinking it may be Charles, she does not think much of it. However, as the movement suddenly becomes more frequent, bright, and erratic, Sara turns to see the incoming lighting storm. Frightened and not knowing what else she could do, Sara's first instinct is to wake Charles from his coma-like state. At first, Sara lightly shakes him, hoping he will wake up, though it does not work, especially considering the turbulence they have been experiencing. Despite her failed attempt, she continues to try various ways to bring him to life. Yet, none of her attempts seem to work.

"Charles, please," she whispers, thinking it could be their end.

Although they continue to near the runway despite the danger lurking outside the aircraft, Sara feels like they will be in an accident in the coming seconds. As the plane tilts, Sara's attention fixes on the nearing lighting strikes. They draw closer before she and those around her hear the terrifying sound of thunder, a bright flash of raw energy, and the enormous tremor that rocks the entire cabin. For a long moment, Sara believes that the plane is about to crash into the airport below. However, she is soon comforted through the frequent and constant flicker of lighting as Charles's hand gently sits atop hers. She turns to him, seeing he has fixated on something outside their plane.

The cabin jolts again, leaving Sara to jump a little in her seat. However, Charles's expression remains the same before surprisingly softening as his attention focuses on some fixed point.

"Sara, we made it," he says, hoping to put her at ease.

She looks at him in pure disbelief.

"We made it," Charles says again. "Have a look."

Sara and Charles look through the small window. While outside has become tremendously dark, only lit by the lighting provided by the airport and the swift-moving storm overhead, they can still make out the basics. The building's structure and ported aircrafts, and the technicians tucked away from the strikes.

"We made it," Sara states, relieved. "What do we do now?"

"It won't take long for this to disperse, and they'll let us off in a minute," Charles states, sure of himself.

Sara nods, unable to do anything else. She soon turns and looks about the plane and at everyone who panicked as she was moments ago. They turn to each other, trying to comfort one another before the flight attendants come over, explaining that they cannot do anything to help get them off the craft.

"How long do you think that'll be?" Sara presses.

"As you can tell, the storms recently haven't been the same as they used to be," he says. "But.... If I'm right, should be right about now."

A split second after Charles had predicted the end of the electrical storm, the flash of incoming strikes finally ceases. The long silence makes the passengers uncertain, though it proves to be short-lived. Once they realize the lightning stopped, everyone cheers and clamors. Sara looks at Charles, and her chest ultimately caves.

"What is it?" he asks, seeing her weary expression.

"I don't think I like flying," Sara says seriously. "Why were we doing this again? Why would anyone risk it?"

Charles turns away, trying to hide the fact that he is chuckling softly. However, he seems to be failing quite miserably. As the humor soon dies, he returns his gaze to her worried personality. She sits with her full attention fixed on him, waiting for an outside perspective.

"Well, they're probably trying to get back to their families," Charles points out.

"Yeah, family.... It seems about right," she agrees, seeing the humanity behind their decision.

Sara and Charles allow the silence to fill the space between them. They sit awkwardly, not permitting their eyes to meet in fear of an additional seemingly strained conversation. However, the tension is soon dissolved as the handful of fight attendants come into view. While they still appear rattled by the dangerous landing, each emanates happiness and peace. The female attendant Sara had encountered while Charles was asleep steps forward, standing in the center of the aisle beside Sara. As Charles and Sara believe she is about to speak, the familiar sound of the plane's P.A. system captures their attention.

"Hi again. It's your captain, Captain Marcel. I'm glad to inform you that we will be disembarking the plane in moments. If you grab your luggage, form a single file line in the aisle to your side, and follow your designated flight attendant to the exit, we will soon be safely inside the airport before moving on to wherever you will be calling home. Thank you all for your patience," the captain announces.

Sara stands and instinctively reaches for their luggage above. As she realizes that the baggage has become stuck within the compartment, Sara tugs almost violently on them, jerking them free. However, they are heavier than Sara remembered. She lowers the bags to her side. Once she allows herself to settle, Sara's eyes rest on Charles.

"Is this normal?" she questions. "I mean, I don't think this was a normal flight. I'm not just talking about the insane weather either."

"I honestly don't know," he replies, taking his bag. "Maybe they saw something we didn't."

Charles manages to slide in beside Sara, forming a line as instructed. However, once he gains the spot beside Sara, Charles slowly realizes his thought may be correct. Yet, he finds himself worrying over the fact he is inadvertently terrorizing Sara. Thinking that his assumption very likely seems to be the case, Charles decides it may be better for Sara to believe that the only pressing danger is the threat of another weather-related anomaly.

"It has to be the storm," Charles states. "They must think it'll come back…. Pilots are trained in meteorology before they're permitted to fly."

"Yeah, I guess that makes sense," she agrees. "But you know your way around the weather yourself. You don't think it will come back, do you?"

"No, I don't," he answers shortly.

Sara finds comfort in Charles's observations. However, she continues to worry about the situation they are in. The danger appears to follow them. Sara had not known Charles for long before agreeing to tag along with him to Washington despite having no idea why they were present. Yet, while they lack the communication that Sara wishes to have, Sara senses with her heightened empathetic ability that Charles needs her for a matter of extreme importance. Even if the extreme importance becomes lost to her, Sara must aid Charles through this time. Yet, curiosity soon gets the better of Sara. Following a man into danger naturally causes frustrations she can avoid with communication.

"Hey Charles, while we're speaking of storms, I still don't get why we're here in Washington."

"I told you why we needed to be here," Charles claims.

Sara allows her eyes to gently lock upon him, though he can tell by her blank expression that more will follow. He is right. Sara turns, facing Charles as her shoulders seem to over-relax while she gradually swings the bag onto one of them.

"You said that *we need to go to Washington. We might be able to stop the storms from there,*" Sara says. "I don't see how, but I still followed you here."

"You did," Charles acknowledges.

Sara stands, staring at Charles. She waits for the explanation she seeks. However, Charles still leaves her in the dark regarding the weather phenomena and its secrets. Once Sara realizes that Charles does not intend to enlighten her about what will follow, her focus returns to where the flight attendant awaits them. As the blonde stewardess turns to see something neither Charles nor Sara can, the cabin can hear the relieving sound of the exit door releasing its airlock before opening. A sigh of relief comes from all on board in a wave, causing Sara to smile.

"Ladies and gentlemen, if you would follow us," the flight attendant says.

Sara, Charles, and everyone aboard slowly shuffle towards the door. However, Sara's mind screams within herself, wanting nothing more than for all to speed the process along. Despite the urge to try anything to do such a thing, Sara sluggishly follows the woman to the exit. Once reaching the top of the attached staircase, Sara checks to see if Charles has remained glued to her side. She quickly descends after finding Charles stays close behind, putting her at ease.

THE COLD FROM THE STREET seemed to follow Sara and Charles into the clean, polished concrete hotel lobby. However, Sara is pleased that the dark exterior has entered the interior. The area around them is considered plain, but it is bright. White is comforting to Sara. She wishes to leave the constant darkness behind. Yet, despite the white and evenly lit space, Sara's mind is continuously forced to endure and relive the horrid experience that brought her here.

"I think my first flight will be my last," Sara announces to Charles. He looks over to her.

"Was it?" he asks. "You had a passport ready to go."

"There was a time when I wanted to travel. I'm over that. I thought I would die the entire time," Sara reasons. "Not that you would know. You were practically unconscious."

Charles smirks as they slow at the center of the room. He pivots to face her. Sara stares at him, waiting to see what he will do next. However, it is not what she expected. Charles nods, acknowledging that he has heard her before he reaches out for her bag.

"Here, let me take that. I'll check us in. You go try to relax," Charles says without thinking.

"What?" Sara begins. "You sure?"

As an answer, his hand finally manages to grasp the handle of her luggage. Charles lifts it and allows it to almost sprawl across his back. Sara unconsciously sways, mirroring Charles as he compensates for the weight. However, she stops once Charles's stance finally becomes sure.

"Yeah, I'm sure. I think you could use it," Charles finishes.

"Oh, well.... Thank you," Sara says awkwardly.

As the words leave Sara's mouth, Charles lightly steps away, heading toward the front desk. While Sara takes a moment to breathe, her gaze drifts through the space around her. There was nothing in the hotel she would not see back in New York. Plain furniture, plants, and halls lead to the hotel's restaurant and bar. In this moment and thought, Sara's feet instantly shuffle to the hallway. She soon enters the hotel bar to see an almost empty, clinically white, steel interior and a single man sitting over by the bartender. Sara draws closer to the men, wanting to sit by the bar. As she nears, the bartender's focus lifts. He greets her with a smile as she takes a seat.

"What can I get for you, Miss?" the bartender asks.

"Ah, I'm not a strong drinker... So, something weaker," she replies, unsure.

"Sure thing," he answers, stepping away.

Once the man begins fixing a drink, Sara's focus shifts to her hands and allows her mind to drift. Yet her break from reality is soon broken. The man seated beside her leans in toward her. However, Sara does not lift her head to face him. Sara's sight remains fixated on her hands, though she spots his beside hers.

"Difficult day?" the man asks.

Sara starts to consider how to answer. However, it does not seem like she can. The man's arm swings through the air, cutting her off before Sara can begin. Yet, Sara does not look at him. She does not want to start anything. Unfortunately, this man has other plans.

"It must have been. After all, you're not a drinker. Yet here you are. Right here, in a bar."

Sara does not respond. Instead, she restricts her breaths and fiddles with her fingers. The short silence is interrupted as the bartender returns and places the soft-colored drink before her. She finally lifts her eyes from their fixed point and trains on the seemingly kind drink maker.

"Thank you," she says.

"No problem," the bartender dismisses before looking at the man.

Sara still avoids the man, sensing nothing from him except pure anger and hatred. However, she also gathers from the expression on the bartender that he does not appreciate the man's presence either. Perhaps it is because of the conversation she interrupted by entering the room.

"I've had a long and difficult day myself.... Long, hard few weeks," the man continues. "I've accomplished so much in such little time.... Finally done what I set out to do a long time ago."

Although Sara remains reserved, the man's statement almost forcefully pulls her attention toward him. Before their eyes met, Sara could sense the lack of fulfillment that came from him. However, Sara is distracted by the dark, sunken appearance that washed over him. The man leans forward, allowing his long black hair to fall into his green eyes. Yet, Sara cannot focus on all his physical attributes. The horrible state of his breath keeps her mind occupied.

"I did right by my father. I'm doing right by my fellow man," he slurs.

"Sounds noble," Sara mutters.

"Yes.... Yes. Yes! It is noble!" the man bellows.

Sara and the bartender pull away from the man. He is intense. The man is being more difficult than Sara can endure after multiple near-death experiences in one afternoon. She tries not to think about that. Instead, Sara fights the burning in her throat after drinking the entirety of her beverage.

"How much?" she eventually asks.

"On the house," he declares, taking the glass.

Before stepping away, the bartender momentarily looks at the man beside Sara. The bartender does not appear enthused. However, he still must do his job and do right by this man.

"Will that be all, Sir?" the bartender asks.

Sara can not help but turn and watch as the man sluggishly looks at him. The distant yet somehow focused tint in his eye, the twisted smile and the disgruntled demeanor overwhelm Sara and the hotel worker. Yet, neither one of them says anything. They only wait for the man to answer.

"Another drink," he replies.

"I think that you may have had enough.... Perhaps a cup of coffee, Sir," the bartender offers.

"Another drink," the man repeats.

The drink maker nods and heads for the various drinks further away. However, before the bartender could return, the man edges his chair closer to Sara's, adding to the intense and uncomfortable situation. Unfortunately, she does not feel comfortable leaving the bar without anyone. She feels safer knowing the bartender is there and can step in.

"Why was your day horrible?" he asks.

"I don't want to talk about it," Sara replies.

She hoped to stop the conversation before it could begin. Despite Sara's wishes, it will proceed as the man laughs, gestures the air with his hands, and leaves his mouth open as though the words were already forming. However, Sara assumes this is the man's mind moving faster than his body can.

"A woman.... that respects her boundaries.... I like that. Tell me, what's—? What's your name?" the man asks.

Sara pauses for a moment, considering ignoring the man. However, she feels like something lies behind what comes next. It compels her to continue despite her better thoughts telling her not to proceed.

"It's Sara. My name is Sara," she reveals.

The man tilts his head back as if savoring the name. Yet, this could be because of his delayed responses. Either way, Sara knows this man will remember through this haze. She can sense the surge of emotions and what she assumes are unpleasant thoughts emanating from him.

"Sara.... Sara, that's a lovely name. It's nice to meet you, Sara," the man begins. "I'm Scott. Scott Davenport."

CHAPTER FIVE

Mr. Davenport's breaths become labored while he unintentionally sways on his stool. For a moment, Sara believes he may fall as a result. However, as his luck may have it, no such thing happens. Mr. Davenport remains firmly seated, allowing the bartender to grant him the drink Mr. Davenport had demanded. The men do not speak; Mr. Davenport only nods and drinks the dark brown liquid. Although Sara is in the conversation and near the man to her right, her mind continuously pulls to the exit. She wants to leave this seemingly toxic environment that Mr. Davenport appears to produce. Yet, something deep inside Sara compels her to stick with the overly strained and tense conversation between herself and Mr. Davenport. She believes there is something more than what appears.

"It's nice to meet you too," Sara replies practically through her teeth.

Sara's response seems to take him a moment to register. However, once Mr. Davenport grasps her simple statement, his head appears to bob, throwing Sara off. Though she does not allow this benign action to change what she is doing, she continues to attempt a decent discussion with the man. As she reopens her mouth and takes a moment to mentally prepare herself for what may happen next and what she may say, Mr. Davenport cuts her off before she can begin.

"So, what brings you to this little slice of hell?" Mr. Davenport asks.

Sara does all she can to ignore the spillage across the bar and on her. After taking a seemingly short breath, Sara wipes the residual liquor onto the paper napkin before her. She does not think much of the alcohol. Sara is busy considering how to answer him.

"I'm here to help a friend," she eventually answers.

"Oh? You're a good friend. Most people would have left them to work things out for themselves," Mr. Davenport states. "I'm going to tell you why I'm here— You won't believe though. I'm here to save the world."

While she could put this extreme claim down as something random and insufficient that a drunk would say to sway a crowd or to impress someone special, Sara knows he is telling the truth due to their crisis and Sara's empathic ability. However, it is like Sara is speaking to Charles. Whatever comes from Mr. Davenport's mouth next will be a riddle she cannot solve.

"I've been.... contracted by the government to, ah.... To fix the whole uncontrollable weather problem thing we've been having," he begins to divulge. "I've fixed part of the problem, but know it's a matter of taming something that doesn't wish to be con-con— *Contained* and controlled."

Sara's expression perks up, and her focus sharpens as she leans toward him. "You work for the government? Are you one of those guys shooting rockets into orbit?" Sara cannot help but question.

Mr. Davenport appears to cut through the daze the alcohol has on him as his eyes become clear. He is surprised. However, Sara can pick up on something else. It is almost like regret. Despite the misery, Mr. Davenport's mainly proud and arrogant stature presses on.

The overconfident man before them leaves Sara and the bartender in an awkward state. They do not know whether it would be wise to speak their opinion or to remain silent, allowing Mr. Davenport a chance to gloat. However, Sara faces the fear that she may have to make another tremendous effort to maintain the current flow of discussion. Luckily, she was granted more delightful commentary by the charming Mr. Davenport.

"Yes, I am.... I'll be the one you'll— You'll thank me for saving your life," Mr. Davenport says, partially to reassure his drunken self.

As Mr. Davenport appears to plan on speaking again, Sara and the mixologist enduring his uncomfortable blabbering are genuinely surprised by Davenport's sudden collapse. Sara pauses. She is shocked. However, she pushes through this and comes to his side, checking on him. He is alive, but Sara assumes he is unconscious from the liquor.

"Is he alright?" the bartender asks, coming around.

"I think so," Sara replies. "What do we do with him?"

The bartender pauses. It stresses Sara. However, he will put her at ease. He deals with this often, more since the worldwide weather phenomena. Everyone ended up like Mr. Davenport.

"I'll call security and escort Scott to his room, where he'll sleep this off," he answers.

Sara turns away from Mr. Davenport's blacked-out and unevenly sprawled body and looks at the bartender. He already has a phone in hand. Before she can respond, the bartender begins to type.

"Thanks for checking on him. I'll take care of him until they get here," the bartender says as he leans down by Mr. Davenport. "Enjoy your stay."

"Are you sure?" she asks.

Although she was expecting some form of reconsideration from the bartender, he only nodded, confirming his kind gesture.

"Alright. Well, thanks for the drink," Sara acknowledges.

"Don't mention it. I figured you had enough to deal with....," the bartender justifies.

Sara's eyes gradually closed before painfully rolling to the back of her head. In this somewhat relaxed state, she nods, unable to do anything except agree with his observations. She slowly comes to rise, lightly squeezing his shoulder in an act of kindness as she does so. Despite the unconscious man she is leaving to be cared for, Sara is being driven toward Charles by a statement made by the same seemingly insane man.

She thinks of how Mr. Davenport works under the government's guidance to secure the globe's weather phenomena, then to Charles and his beliefs that Washington is the best location for the same cause. As she heads back to the hotel lobby, her focus slowly drifts to the snow-engulfed street. Although she was gone for only a short time, the entirety of the road was blanketed in thickening ice and not a light and slow cast as one would initially expect.

"Now, when did that happen?" she asks.

However, the thought of the snowy exterior is soon lost as she turns around to see Charles gazing upon her. Charles lightly strides across the icy concrete and to Sara's side while he rubs his arm for warmth. Yet, just as he reaches her, his attention is broken by the two burly security guards heading for the bar area from which Sara came.

"What's that about?" Charles asks.

"A drunk, they're going to take him to his room," Sara effortlessly replies.

"Oh," he breathes in response.

A brief silence passes. Neither one knows how to fill it. However, Charles looks about, trying to find something to say. He does not want anything between them. Unfortunately, he does not get much of a say in this matter. They do not know each other. They only agreed to come here together to settle the uncontrollable weather. With this, Charles realizes there is something he can say.

"Ah, here," Charles says, handing Sara her hotel room key. "I figured you could use this."

"Yeah…. I could. Thanks, Charles," Sara softly acknowledges.

Charles notices her distant expression and the dark emptiness behind her eyes. Charles becomes taken aback, fearing whatever has gripped Sara in her short time away from him. His feet unintentionally take a step back in a small act of defense. However, his thoughts go to his mouth as it is dry, and his eyes slant.

"What is it?" Charles asks, frightened of the answer.

Agony rises deep within Charles as Sara does not answer him. She has caught him in a time of personal distress. It is an unfortunate emotion the pair of them have picked up on, leading to a more prompt answer for him.

"I'm still just wondering why it had to be Washington," Sara eventually states.

Although Charles could understand where Sara was coming from, it did not stop the disappointment from becoming fixated upon his face. He knows it is a big ask of her. To ask her to come along to the other side of the country for a reason she does not fully understand. His chest becomes heavy, hands form into semi-fists, and he breaths slowly as Charles realizes the struggle he faces.

"Look, Sara.... I don't know what to tell you. I don't...." Charles claims. "If I told you everything...."

"Is it because of the weather satellites? Because of the program they have here?" Sara continues to push.

Charles pauses, unsure whether he is somewhat impressed or surprised. However, he struggles to answer Sara's query. He continues to fight his inner thoughts and reservations, thinking he will put her in harm's way. As the concept of Sara hurt and the image of the Great Goddess reemerges, Sara unexpectedly nods, almost hurt by Charles's lack of communication. With a confused and emotionally damaged look from Charles, Sara turns and walks toward the exit.

"Sara, wait," Charles says as she reaches the door.

She obeys and turns to face him. Sara does not know what she expects from this, but she knows Charles must work past whatever looms over his head. He must tell her what he is hiding and how it affects her.

"Wait for what, Charles? I followed you all the way here with practically nothing to go on. I know you're hiding so much from me. I can feel it. But I also know you need me for something and that it's bigger than you're letting on," Sara says. "All I've asked you are simple questions. Which I think is fair."

"They are fair...... I just— I don't know if it'll be too much for you. I don't know if you're ready," he excuses.

Sara stares at Charles, still waiting for him to allude her to what is happening. Unfortunately, he remains silent. Sara's empathetic abilities are not enough for her. She cannot read his mind, and she needs to know.

"Charles, you need to start explaining things to me. I can't stay here if I can't even trust the person I'm helping," she demands. "I know you're a good man, but you're troubled— It's why I came."

Charles freezes again, thinking her ultimatum through. However, Sara does not seem to see this long moment of hesitation as Charles does. Her hand rests on the exit as she tries to leave again. She cannot keep playing his games.

"Alright. Alright, but not here. We'll say nothing here. It's not safe," Charles agrees. "Upstairs. We'll talk upstairs. I'll explain everything."

"Okay," she says, acknowledging his prevision.

CHARLES HAD KEPT HIS hotel room of choice simple. The space they have walked into is barely lit and empty. However, he instantly makes himself physically comfortable as he is more than aware that the following conversation between Sara and himself will be rough. He places himself on the bed, gently resting his back against the bedhead, crossing his foot on top of the other, and signals for Sara to sit.

"Come on, let's get this over with," Charles begins.

"Yeah, alright," she replies heavily.

She slowly walks over to the small, hideous beige couch directly across from Charles and hesitantly takes her place. While she had asked Charles to explain himself, Sara has distanced herself from him as she does not know where the following conversation will take them. Being nervous, Sara momentarily plays with the lining of her shirt before finding the courage to lift her gaze to Charles. Despite expecting Charles to immediately find a way to resist telling her everything she wishes to know, as he has done previously, she oddly is faced with a seemingly patient and somewhat confident man.

"Where do you want to begin? What do you want to know?" Charles asks.

Charles is not messing around. He must know what it is that Sara wishes to learn. However, Sara's mind is sluggish. She tries to find some way to respond in a way that leaves Charles to explain all she must know. To find a way to ask something she had been curious about since first meeting Charles. Yet, Sara's thoughts continue to run blank, and her stomach churns in nervousness.

"Ah.... I'm not sure where to begin," Sara admits.

Charles chuckles dryly while his head rolls to the side. He did not know what he expected from Sara. She does not know anything. How could she know where to start? She does not even know what the start is.

"I guess it would be hard to choose when you already don't know much.... There's a fair bit to know. I'm sorry about that," Charles apologizes. "But I guess you would want to know why I ended up in New York and why I'm here now."

"Well, is New York the beginning?" Sara asks reasonably.

Charles takes a breath. The weight of her minimalistic question is more than she realizes. However, Charles knows it is something that she must know going forward. Unfortunately, it does mean he can permit himself to continue. Yet, Charles tries to move ahead and keep going.

"New York is where I was looking for a.... *solution* to a problem.... It's not the beginning, no," Charles replies.

Sara falls silent. She had not known the full extent of Charles's issues. However, Sara will know the drastic side of his origins in the coming moments. Yet, she remains oblivious to the weight of these issues and whether there is a valid reason for Charles's reservations.

"What is the beginning?" she continues.

"A trip to Brazil," he replies. "The reason to why isn't important.... But I ended up in Brazil, and I met her followers."

"Who's followers?" Sara says, feeling the need to ask.

Charles's eyes linger on Sara as he momentarily reconsiders revealing the truth to her. However, once he realizes there is no other option than to be completely honest, Charles's head dips to his feet before he stands. He walks over to the window and peers through the blinds to the street below as though it holds the answers to his troubles. It takes him a second to conquer his internal struggles and explain the impossible.

"The Great Goddess's," he eventually answers. "Her followers.... They saw the unstable state I was in and my *potential*. They brought me back to what they called their home, their sacred space. It's where I met her, the Great Goddess. She showed me all these things like I showed you back in New York. Her throne— Her stationed space. It's where I learned and studied the natural order of things, like how to read the Earth and work alongside it."

"Goddess? What's she the Goddess of exactly?" she wonders.

"Earth and nature," Charles states. "You've heard of her before, but you just don't realize it.... Perhaps you'll recognize her by her more *traditional* namesake, as Mother Nature."

Charles slowly turns toward Sara, wanting to see her reaction firsthand. He would have expected some form of astonishment. However, Charles assumes she is drawing from her empathetic abilities, experiencing the same emotional reactions as Charles himself. After a brief moment of silence from Charles and Sara, he realizes she is still waiting for him to continue.

"She then soon took me in as her.... Ah, second in command, if it were. She taught me everything I know. She taught me that her life is tied to this Earth in a way that is difficult to explain. She is tied to the land and the elements, and with her away from her station, the world erupted into chaos— The storms that have been destroying the world," he quickly clarifies. "This is where my journey to New York comes into play, and things get complicated. You see, the role of Mother Nature is a matter of ability and responsibility. And I was looking for someone to succeed the title."

Although Sara knows Charles is telling the truth, she almost cannot acknowledge what he divulges. Sara's lips purse, legs crossed, and arms fold over one another in a sudden act of defense. However, he does not seem to mind Sara's trouble with the information that he has given. It is more than understandable not to believe after being told tall tales of folklore and the importance of your part in such a claim.

"You were looking for *someone to succeed the title*?" Sara repeats.

"Yes," he answers in short. "You."

The room falls silent. Nothing is noticeable in the tense situation. Sara allows her arms to slip away from the other in a moment of self-reflection. However, the sight of Sara's discomfort causes Charles to be in an equally disturbed emotional state.

He thinks he may have to find a way to comfort the woman he barely knows. His lips part as Charles attempts to find something to say. However, he cannot. Luckily, Sara is willing to contribute to the awkward and dense discussion.

"You're saying it's.... Me? Me of all people?" Sara questions. "Why? What makes me so special?"

"It's your natural ability.... It's one of the main qualities that make up the Great Goddess. All that came before her possessed the same power," Charles claims. "It is a gift from the divine, preparing you for a more.... Suitable role."

"No. No, that can't be right," Sara dismisses. "That's not right. It's not me."

"But, it is. It is right," Charles reassures. "And I brought you here to help me stop the intervention that made the chaos that nearly killed us on that plane...... The military took the Great Goddess from her station in the Amazon. All in an attempt to separate her from the Earth, from her nature-bending ability. She's all that stands in the way and prevents them from controlling the Earth's atmosphere. It will eventually kill everyone. It might stabilize the weather, but that doesn't stop man from killing the planet that we live on. Where there's no planet, there's no people."

Sara nods, finding most of what Charles had said to be of reason and understanding. However, she pauses, thinking over something specific that Charles had said for a moment longer. She instantly finds the connection without the constant and disturbing haze that Sara had undergone for the last segment of the conversation.

However, whether or not it is significant does not matter when she is in the dark with manners that are paramount. Yet, Sara yearns for honest responses regarding this newfound information. Leaving her to nothing more than see out for those semi-logical answers.

"Wait, you said the military?" she asks. "As in the American military?"

Charles's expression and mind click, realizing she is angling at something. However, he dreads what comes his way more than he expected. Unfortunately, there is reason for him to worry.

"Like Mr. Davenport?" Sara questions.

At this moment, Charles's eyes enlarge, and his chest tightens in anger and fear while his mouth continues to reform, attempting to find something suitable to say while thinking of the madman who had taken the Great Goddess herself.

CHAPTER SIX

Amongst the overwhelming fury that burns from deep within Charles, he faces nothing more than bewilderment at the knowledge that Sara has somehow obtained. He wonders how she could have learned the name that has ruined so many lives, including his own. This man of power, anger, and misguided attempts at global stabilization had managed to socialize to such a grand scale to learn of Sara. The woman prophesized to take on the role of the Goddess of nature.

"How-how....? How could you possibly know of Mr. Davenport?" Charles eventually finds the courage to ask.

Sara is frightened. She did not think Charles would act this way. However, Sara did not know he would have any connection to Mr. Davenport. Yet, Charles has only told her the basics about him. Perhaps Mr. Davenport is someone from his past, someone Charles did not believe he would bump into.

"You know him too?" Sara questions.

The darkening tint behind Charles's eye is enough to tell Sara so. Yet, how they know each other is another mystery that only Charles can allude her to. From the greying tone that emanates from Charles, Sara realizes that Mr. Davenport is not worth dealing with. Leaving her to both want more information about this strangely deranged man and simultaneously distance herself as far as she can from him. As she wants to change the subject, thinking it may be for the best, she notes how Charles has begun to struggle.

"Yeah.... I know him. He's the guy behind taking the Great Goddess. He had a vendetta against her and used the opportunity the government gave him to his twisted advantage," Charles painfully reveals.

"I'm so sorry, I had no idea," Sara apologizes.

Charles pulls his attention away from Sara, evidently lost in an internal conflict. Despite his troubles, Charles manages to cut through unnecessary thoughts and complicated emotions and then regains his focus on how Sara knows of the monster he is fighting against.

"How do you know him, Davenport?" Charles wonders, trying desperately to contain his rage.

Sara notices his struggles. While she knows the emotional battle Charles is fighting, Sara does not know how to act. She sees his anger and wonders if she should tell him. Things might not turn out well if she were to say something.

However, Sara decides to tell him, thinking it may help Charles with whatever he is dealing with. Yet, she still fears his reaction and the damage this may inflict.

"Well.... He— Ah, I met him in the bar downstairs. He was the drunk I told you about," Sara discloses. "I didn't think much of it.... I thought what he did was more important than who he was."

"He's here!" Charles stresses.

The seethe overrunning the room makes Sara flinch from his intensity. However, she settles, seeing Charles forcefully containing himself, slowly recomposing himself despite the haunting troubles that seem to follow and overrun him.

"Well.... I suppose it's not the worst thing to happen," Charles begins. "He could be of some use while he's here...."

Sara is slow to respond. Her focus is on the growing emotional turmoil that comes from Charles, gradually extending to her, changing her view on the current topic. Despite the discussion, Sara fixates on

Charles for a moment, finding behind his anger lies fear and sadness. However, the full power and the combination of Charles's woes soon become overwhelming and drown her ability to think clearly.

It leaves her staring at Charles, hoping he may either continue at his current pace or explain to her what he means. However, Charles's mind is distant, making Sara's hopes slim. Yet, Charles proves to be persistent despite his mind being in disarray and brought to the singular thought of the Great Goddess.

"We could wait, find out what floor he's staying on, eventually follow him back to wherever he has been working out of.... The hole that he's crawled out of," Charles eventually states himself rather than Sara. "What.... What do you think?"

It takes Sara longer than she would have wished to realize that Charles had asked her opinion. Though, the moment she does, her entire body practically jumps as she is unsure of herself. Sara settles for a minute, thinking over Charles's proposal. While it is simple, Sara does not know if she could think of a better plan as she is unaware of all that has transpired and the continuously rising dangers that come with the territory.

"Well.... Do you think it will work?" she asks.

Something flashes behind Charles's eyes, revealing his reservations and doubts about his self-concocted plan. However, as the seconds pass, Charles seems to reassure himself, regain confidence with the partial idea, and possibly restore what Davenport took. Sara then notes how Charles rests his head on an angle as if thinking of something else behind his thought of armature pursuit and mild stalking.

"Well, actually, I think it'll save me some time.... I was wondering how to narrow more than a few things down," Charles admits. "Having him here.... I'll be able to track him and find the things I need to know before trying to prevent the final launch.... The final launch with all the modifications that they need."

"Oh.... It's handy, I guess," Sara unintentionally mutters.

The silence returns almost instantly, leaving an unbearable tension between them and sweat to build between Charles's shoulder blades. In the uncomfortable ambiance, Sara finds herself allowing this time of silence to bring her ultimately bring clarity. She thinks through what Charles must do in the coming days and what she knows that she must also do in support. However, it additionally brings about various and other disturbing realizations.

"What about me?" Sara asks.

Charles freezes, perplexed and wondering what Sara means. He looks into Sara's eyes like they would allude to what he must know. However, while Charles knows there is something more behind what Sara asked. He will not figure it out himself.

"I'm sorry. What about you....?" Charles questions.

"You'll track him, find out everything he does like you said you would, right? And then run into wherever he's been working and hiding himself, find your Goddess, and do whatever else you need to do," Sara begins. "But, what is it you need me for? You want me to take over or for this Goddess, but that doesn't seem to do with anything you'll be doing. So, what about me?"

Charles lets a chuckle break the uncomfortable sense that engulfs the room before bringing his attention to Sara and her worry about what lies ahead. He knows convincing Sara to agree to something illegal, somewhat unethical, and almost insane will be impossible, especially since he already knows the answer. It causes Charles to do nothing more than stand there, trying to fathom a way to explain things to her while somehow leaving Sara to believe his plan to be of some sound.

"Well...... The thing is, I do need you to come with me," Charles claims. "You'd understand more once we would make it inside wherever Davenport has been hiding himself."

Sara's face flushes. She has had enough of his games. However, this does not mean Charles will let her in.

"Charles, I don't understand now. Right now, which is the problem I was talking to you about," Sara presses. "Why? Why do I need to follow you? What else is there? What else are you not telling me?"

Their eyes remained locked on the other's, trying to communicate almost emotionally. However, this stops as Charles pulls his gaze to his quivering hands. His heartbeat fastens before his mouth twitches because of Charles's growing worry. Luckily, Charles manages to turn away from his frightened and slightly pained hands and then swiftly notes how he unintentionally taps his foot onto the floor. As he stops his habitable fidgeting, Charles finds the words.

"Because.... Sara, I need you to take the helm, to take the raw power," he says, seeming somewhat exasperated.

Sara looks at Charles like he is crazy. However, she takes a page out of Charles's book and lazily drops her line of sight to her hands. She finds herself grateful for this momentarily glimpse of distance and clarity even though she knows it must be short-lived in their predicament. The seriality and stress of what is next to come slowly compress within her chest, eventually leaving Sara with constricted breaths and severely pained fingertips.

"And how do we do that?" she asks.

"You'll need to...... you'll need to be where it was that they took the Great Goddess's power," Charles says without mentioning the most horrible aspects of his true meaning.

Sara can see there is something he has not mentioned. However, Sara wants to give him a chance. She can feel him struggling to let her in and tell her things that will make them both uncomfortable.

"Is that all we need to do?" she presses.

There is a beat of silence as Charles thinks. The slight gap in conversation causes Sara more distress despite her best efforts to remain calm. Her heartbeat continues to rise, and her lip sweats from pure nerves. Although it is uncomfortable, it lets Sara inhale as she sits upright.

"More or less," Charles whispers.

Sara's eyes remain locked, attempting to see what Charles keeps from her. However, she knows it is useless. The emotion she picks up on from him is reserved and opposed to what she is accustomed to with Charles, such as anger, panic, fear, and depression.

"More or less?" Sara repeats.

Before he opens his mouth, Charles is disappointed in himself. He knows he will not answer her how she needs him to. Yet, it does not stop him from making this mistake. Charles falls into fears and anxieties.

"Yeah," he confirms in short.

The short burst of rage on Sara's part dies, allowing her to think without taking her frustrations out on Charles. However, she still believes the only way to ease her troubles is through the explanation that she seeks. She must understand.

"Does that mean anything in particular, or is that something you're waiting for me to figure out at the last minute? I'll probably be with you in some government-watched space that Mr. Davenport frequents, with what I assume to be armed men." Sara asks reasonably.

Charles inhales deeply, hands twitch, and his eyes instinctively shut in the uncomfortable confutation that he faces, knowing that she speaks the truth and what he is more than aware that she fears. He soon finds the spirit to reopen his eyes and fix them on Sara's deepening seriousness. However, it does not stop the uneasy feeling in his stomach.

"I was trying to keep that to myself," Charles says. "See, I know it will be a much for you…. To see what it is that's waiting for you. Especially considering what I'm asking of you, Sara. The responsibility I would bestow on you, the things you would see. It's on top of the extended and restricted life that you'll live…."

Charles pauses, thinking of a way to continue as he has become slightly unstable and cannot control his wavering hands. Frightened that Sara may notice, Charles instinctively tucks them deep into his pockets, hoping to hide them from her. He takes a single step forward, wanting to be clear in the point he tries to get across, though Charles struggles with Sara staring up at him. She is still waiting for him to continue.

"Don't get me worry, Sara.... It's a gift I'll be offering you, but I won't lie. I knew the Great Goddess for a very, very long time. I knew of all the things that came with it. I mean it when I say it's something wonderful, but it's also, unfortunately, a burden," Charles explains.

The pleading and agonizing pain lingers in his eyes from the thought of the Great Goddess, leaving Sara to wallow in Charles's gut-wrenching memories. However, she manages to cut past the rush of his emotional trauma and see the truth in his statement and what lies within.

"Charles, in case you haven't noticed, everything in life is both a gift and a burden.... All I've asked is for you to tell me what's happening and what I should expect in any situation you decide to walk me into. You want to stroll me into Davenport's workspace to look for whatever you're looking for in there," Sara says, dismissing his argument points. "What else is there that I need to know?"

Charles's chest pounds. He does not how Sara will take what he has to tell her. Charles is scared that she will not move forward with him once she understands what it will entail. However, it is a risk he must take at some point.

"It's.... It's ugly," Charles warns.

Sara exhales and looks directly at Charles, informing him of her growing impatience toward him. Despite this, Charles came to sit at the foot of the bed with a sigh. Yet, he does not allow his eyes to meet hers.

"They've separated her from her abilities...... The Great Goddess, I mean— From her connection to everything. But, to connect you to this immense power that comes with the title, you would normally have to be bestowed it by the former," Charles divulges. "Since she and her abilities are no longer attached to the earthly plane, you would need to find where the raw connection ended up because it's too powerful and cosmic. It would be impossible to destroy. You'll need to interact with whatever remains intact with the entity to divert the role of Mother Nature to you."

"And by that, you mean.... Her body?" Sara wonders.

Charles does not answer upon being extremely uncomfortable with the idea himself. He does not know how Sara deals with the unbearable truth of the endless possibilities. It comes with uncharted territory and the privilege of serving the Great Goddess and those affected by her actions.

"Possibly," Charles answers truthfully.

Though the physical space between them is not much, the mental and emotional distance is enough to convince Sara to drop all attempts at conversation. She now sees why Charles did not want to let her know this information.

Sara stands, wanting to leave the conversation and all that has come with it. Yet, it appears as though Charles firmly believes otherwise. However, before Charles can speak again, Sara realizes that she must intervene and disallow him the chance.

"Well.... It seems perfectly logical now, doesn't it?" she begins. "I think I should get bed. I mean, it's been one hell of a day. It took its toll on me. I mean, it must have been for you, right?"

Charles's expression is enough to tell one he is worried and somewhat disappointed. Yet, Sara does not need to make eye contact with him to know this is true. However, she tries to get past it and makes it to the door, but she stops before grabbing the handle. She senses the guilt that comes from Charles and turns, allowing him a chance to get a final word in before she leaves.

"Yeah, it has taken its toll...." Charles begins. "I'm sorry I had to do this to you, Sara. I'm sorry I had to be the one to do this to your life, that things have to be this way. But I do want you to know I'm glad you're next in line for the role of the Great One over everyone else. I can tell that you'll be the one to do good things for the world and those that live in it."

"Thank you, Charles.... It means a lot," Sara acknowledges before finally stepping away.

IT HAD BEEN OVER AN hour since Sara had left his side. However, Charles could think she was being selfish or irrational. After all, her worries, thoughts, opinions, and observations are within reason.

While his thoughts mainly gravitate toward Sara and his time in the rainforest, Charles's priority is the hotel exit. He sits in silence in the far corner of the lobby, hidden behind various planets and an odd bit of furniture. In this position, he can see the elevator hotel guests use, the front desk with the reception staff, and the glass double doors with snow piled against them. As he thinks his current plan may not work based on current events and the weather intervention, men and their snow-plowing gear come into view. They are shoveling away any snow from in front of the building, bringing a smile to his face.

"I don't care if they think it will take a week! I need to be out those doors in five minutes!" a man's voice booms from the opening elevator doors.

Though Charles could not see the man in question, who he had screamed at, or if he was on his phone, Charles did not need to spot the man to identify him. The man's voice had given his identity away. The second the man had stepped out of the mechanical box, Charles fights himself internally to contain his anger and pure hatred. Mr. Davenport furiously stalks across the chilled floor to face the hard-working men on the other side. He impatiently taps on the glass, signaling for them to hurry. Charles is grateful for the generous area dividing them. However, Charles is just as impatient as Mr. Davenport, wanting to reach Mr. Davenport.

CHAPTER SEVEN

Sara did not think things would move this fast. It seemed like only a minute ago that Charles told her about Mr. Davenport and his men hiding out in the warehouse district. Then again, Charles appeared more concerned about the terraforming ceremony Sara would endure and the cargo ship pulling into the Washington harbor. She did not think much about it until Charles pointed out that these ships did not come that far in. However, Sara still wonders how things escalated like this.

Yet, Sara moves past this and looks out the window of their rented car, out to the vast water to see that Charles had not lied about the misplaced cargo ship docked in the harbor. Although the weather has settled down, the surrounding shops, cafes, and restaurants in the waterfront area are empty. It seems like only the occasional pedestrian strides by. It is like they go to great lengths to avoid this particular ship. Yet, while everyone is trying to steer away from the area, Sara cannot help but notice how the boat seems to call to her. Seemingly beckoning to her, begging Sara to step aboard and find whatever it is that is waiting for her.

"What do you think they have on there?" Sara asks, not letting her eyes pull away from the ship.

Charles sighs as he considers what Davenport could need from this freighter. Whether there is something that he needs from the ship or whether it is a means of transportation. These thoughts bring Charles a great deal of misery as he attempts to consider all the viable options Mr. Davenport may have concocted since capturing the Great Goddess.

"I don't know.... I've seen him with helicopters and more than a few Jeeps. He has a pull with the government. I didn't know he had enough to permit this," Charles says.

"What kind of pull lets him do this, though? Why would he need the harbor? For what use?" she questions.

"Well, it means he's close to achieving his goal.... He's going to launch the satellites any day now," Charles assumes.

Sara finally lets her attention slip away from the abomination in the harbor and turns toward Charles's suddenly sickened appearance. His fists instinctively tighten around the steering wheel upon having a sitting weight of vulnerability overwhelming the car as his head lightly tips forward in what Sara could assume to be determination. Through Charles's serial focus, Sara can see the fear and sadness that has gripped him and sense the agony that has begun to tear him down.

"We'll get there.... We'll stop it," Sara says, trying to comfort him. "How far out are we?"

"Not far," he states.

Sara watches his eyes glare at the road ahead like a terrifying predator. For the first time since she's met Charles, she finds herself somewhat fearful of him, of what he could do in this state of mind. Not only has her freight for him come as a first, but Sara is suddenly unable to sense what Charles needs, wants, and feels. As Sara tries to empathize with him, she can only find an empty pit of darkness emanating from him. Perhaps somehow reflecting the conflict that battles within him.

"We're here," Charles announces.

As the car begins to slow, Sara is at a loss and only stares at Charles for this moment. It is as though she had not heard him. Sara appears to press her concentration to find something. As she cannot understand what Charles is undergoing, her mind slowly drifts, wondering how they could have made it here from the harbor as fast as they did. However, she soon brushes these thoughts aside, turning her head to take in the almost extreme ruggedness of the exterior, the seemingly endless supply of armed men guarding the space, and the few security cameras surveilling them.

"This is it?" she asks, somehow disbelieving.

Sara slowly notices how the men guarding the area do not seem to consider the street she and Charles are on and how their focus remains on the property tied to the warehouse and those that move within it. Sara momentarily wonders why that may be, as she thought their purpose was to keep intruders from entering. Sara knows they are watching for something or someone on the compound itself. Despite this strange thought and observation, Sara soon loses interest in what could cause their confusing movements. She then returns her dedication to the man beside her as he opens his mouth for his following answer.

"Yes, this is it.... Took the car with the driver, and we followed him here, watched him walk through that door," Charles says as he nods to the front of the building. "But we'll be going through there."

Sara watches Charles gesture to where the equipment goes and from the side of the warehouse. While she knows this was to calm her nerves and planned to be a supposedly efficient tactic, Sara cannot fully understand his logic as there appear to be more men present than what she found surveilling the space.

"Charles...... Won't they still see us coming?" Sara attempts to caution.

Charles looks at Sara with a strange expression, one that causes Sara to almost recoil from him altogether. It is an odd mix of reassurance and confidence she is not accustomed to with Charles, especially in this moment of insanity and imminent danger. Caught in her fear of the situation and what is currently being induced by Charles, Sara's fingers lightly tremble as she slowly notices the sweat that has started to form just above her lip.

"You're right...... They'll see whoever they come across, particularly whoever they come across first," Charles acknowledges. "That's why I'll be going in, they'll go after me...."

Sara pauses with her expression locked in what appears to be horror upon listening to what Charles says. However, he does not seem concerned by Sara's thoughts. He merely focuses on the warehouse and the men walking through the perimeter. While Charles continues to stare at what they both know to be conflict, Sara begins to search for a way to stress the importance of what it is that his plan will bring.

"Uh, isn't that a problem? What if I need you in there?" Sara asks.

"It's not a problem. It'll get me to where I need to be. To the things, I need to destroy the satellite. After that, I'll come back for you. I'll come back to help you find her and find the power that remains. Then you'll need to leave while I sort things out from there," Charles directs.

"Where the hell do I go? They'll be after me, won't they?" she stresses. "Where could I go that they wouldn't find me?"

A long sigh leaves Charles's mouth, revealing his gradually thinning confidence and patience. Although Sara wishes for nothing more than the answers she seeks, the thought that she may have inadvertently provoked Charles leaves her to pull her feet together nervously. Sara continues to think that she may have further caused an issue between Charles and herself that was not there before. One that may potentially affect what transpires next. However, Charles seems to ignore whatever Sara believes she has done and appears to consider her options.

"Just run, play it as you go, but make sure you're back at the airport by eight," Charles says. "We'll need to leave as soon as possible for...."

"The ceremony?" she wonders aloud.

Charles is uncomfortable. He does not know how to respond. There is not much he could say to her, but now, anything he says can sway Sara's thoughts and decisions. Charles's only option in this situation is to roll with her statement and keep moving on.

"Yeah," Charles answers before turning away.

Before Sara can ask him what the ceremony would entitle and where they would be going for the traditional and power-transforming phenomena, Charles exits the car with his back turned to the warehouse as he appears to fix his jacket. Sara momentarily stares after him with the thought of the airport still fresh on her mind and the truly unbearable trauma that they endured previously. However, Sara seems to stop these unnecessary thoughts from disrupting what they are supposed to be fully committed to as she steps out to join Charles.

"Alright, I'll go in, and then you'll slip in while they're distracted, right?" Charles says as he walks away.

Sara wonders whether it would be better for her to follow him and slip in from behind, hoping they will be more likely to go for Charles over her or to wait for everyone inside to be preoccupied. Yet, her decision halts as Sara suddenly notices a dark figure violently jerk away from a window at the top of the building. For a short moment, Sara is frightened that their plan will not work and attempts to find whatever she saw will not work. However, these thoughts disappear as shouting erupts from where she knows Charles has entered.

"Oh," Sara breathes.

Sara's feet pick up and effortlessly propel her toward the warehouse, to what she knows will be the first of many steps to her ridiculously over-complicated future. As she draws closer to the warehouse, Sara forcefully stops at the entrance. Grateful that Charles had pulled everyone's attention away from it. With many self-encouraging sways, she peers around the door to see that the performance Charles must be giving somewhere within has evacuated almost the entire building.

Sara slowly steps inside, ignoring the few people still working on their assigned tasks. Her feet lightly pulse across the floor, and her focus rests high like she is where she is supposed to be. The majority of the warehouse is what Sara had envisioned, vast and open. However, she is surprised that there appear to be many compartments in the space that surrounds her. Sara's hand rests on the first handle before hearing Charles and numerous men charging into the main work area. She quickly rushes inside to avoid the unnecessary attention she may bring before Sara notices the crashing sound and a few moans of agony uproar from where she knew Charles and the men to be.

"Hang in there," she whispers, knowing Charles will not hear her.

Despite the exciting events on the opposite side of the door, she takes several steps backward before Sara ultimately turns to face a device she could only assume to be the satellite that Charles will be searching for. Sara can only look at it in what she would consider awe, not knowing whether she should go ahead and continue on her way, searching for power. Sara can save Charles time and destroy the mechanical beast before her. As she starts to believe that it would be best to crumble any plans for the satellite, Sara's eyes drift, noting that Mr. Davenport has been watching her.

"I know you.... I do know you, don't I?" Davenport asks, almost dumbfounded.

"I-I don't think you do, no," Sara attempts.

Sara knows that her lie will not be of any substance to Davenport. He does not believe her either. His blank and confused expression has subsided. He now has some level of understanding. Mr. Davenport crosses his arms and lifts his head, revealing the firm stance he could take with her. However, before he affirms his position and seemingly righteous plans to her like Sara would assume, he relaxes, allowing his arms to drop to either side of him, and gently sits on an ideally placed office chair.

"You came in with Charles...." Davenport gathers. "See, after learning as much as I have from him, I didn't think that he would let someone tag along into my place of business.... I took him for someone who would rather have things be more intimate and personal. You must be something rather important, if not to him, then to...."

An uncomfortable silence passes as Mr. Davenport stares at Sara. He has something on his mind, leaving Sara unnerved and guarded. Her instinct is to run. Yet, something else from deep inside compels her to remain firmly planted before him, a primal impulse.

Sara's eyes flicker between the steel-grated staircase and the overly uncomfortable situation with Mr. Davenport. Unfortunately, he notes how she had diverted her eyesight and brings himself to look at the steal door tipped at the top of the staircase. His focus lies there for a long moment, almost like it holds the answer to the decision he attempts to make. Although it seems to give him an entirely different reply than the one he thought. While momentarily pulling his attention away from the locked door, Mr. Davenport finally connects Sara's presence to his work. He knows why she is here and what that means with what remains above them.

"So, you're the one I've been warned of," Davenport concludes while placing his hand on his thigh, and his focus returns to the door.

His almost disinterest in the conversation with Sara ultimately confuses her, making her want nothing more than to know what is behind the door. She wonders whether it is the oversized satellite before her or something benign. Sara even notes how it could be as simple as a trap. The more Sara thinks of all likely scenarios, the more she believes that only danger awaits her. Yet, Sara simultaneously imagines she must see what is behind the steal door herself.

"Sorry?" Sara asks with her mind still sifting through many possible schemes.

"You're the next in line for the role. The next dammed woman tricked into believing she is doing right by the world when she is merely condemning it to death," Davenport almost taunts. "Are you not?"

Sara stepped away from the stance she had taken, the stance that something from within had commanded her to take. She takes another look at the door in question. Sara's mind drifts away from the potential danger she may meet and wonders if it could be the thing she came in to find. Whether it may very well be the power she is supposed to acquire. While this thought continues to run through her, Mr. Davenport seems to have the same idea. His fingers suddenly come to itch toward his plastic access key. Sensing movement, an unidentifiable emotion, and a completely unexpected thought coming from him, Sara stops to return her gaze. However, Sara instinctively finches as Davenport finally pulls the badge from his pocket. Once Sara settles, they both stare at the key.

"How much do you know?" Davenport questions.

While he speaks to Sara, Davenport's eyes remain fixated on the dangling plastic card. He is planning something. Unfortunately, Sara will pay the price for it, no matter what it is. Mr. Davenport is strategic.

"Well, that you plan on launching this thing into orbit.... And a few more unappealing details surrounding you and what you've done," Sara divulges.

Mr. Davenport lets out a deep chuckle and allows an amused smirk to stretch across his face while he lifts his attention to Sara. She looks into his eyes, strangely finding him reserved despite the hatred for what lies behind all the issues between him and what has transpired.

"I'm not the bad that you may think I am in this scenario," Davenport claims.

Sara's mouth opens as if she were about to ask him what he meant. However, he tosses the keycard over to Sara. She catches it with a clap and looks down at it in her hand, obviously caught off guard. Sara's focus returns to Davenport as he softly gestures up the staircase.

"What is this?" Sara questions.

Davenport walks over to his satellite and rests against it, knowing she may never know the truth unless he enlightens. As Sara steps forward, she notices how he appears to inspect the device, yet she knows otherwise. Her feet stop in place as she considers her options. However, Sara cannot help but note how the staircase leads to the top floor. To the floor that had the blurred figure jerked away from the window, or so she had thought. Perhaps what Sara saw was nothing more than a simple movement. As Sara contemplates the possibilities behind the door and what Mr. Davenport could gain from this moment, her feet unsteadily shuffle toward the stairs.

"Is this a trick?" she asks.

Mr. Davenport's expression appears reserved. He does not want to make the situation between them worse. However, he does not think he can make it any better. They posited against one another in the Goddess's war.

"You've been fed misinformation.... The card is something to educate you," Davenport states.

Her eyes momentarily regain contact with Mr. Davenport's before she starts climbing. Sara stops at the top, looking at the scanning device and the card in her hand. She considers stepping down, resuming her pursuit of what remains of the immense power, although something compels her to swipe the key through the small black box. The device instantly recognizes the card in use and lights up the top strip within the console. Finding herself frightened of what may be waiting for her inside, Sara does nothing more than stare at the console before her.

"What are you waiting for?" Mr. Davenport wonders from below.

She momentarily looks down at Davenport, finding nothing except for him exactly where she had left him. Although his eyes growl at her, they remain soft as he maintains his gaze up at Sara, waiting for her to enter the space above. However, they both find that Sara faces an unmeasurable amount of fear. A fear that has almost completely paralyzed her.

"Erm.... Nothing. I'm not waiting for anything," she answers, knowing it is due to her ever-growing terror.

Despite this, Sara manages to lift her hand to the handle. However, her eyes shut as if she were trying to find something to help her through this unknown endeavor. Once Sara eventually opens the door, her eyes reopen and focus on the dark space. Though she initially finds nothing worth noting, Sara soundlessly steps inside, thinking it is significant.

CHAPTER EIGHT

The chill in the air from this perpetual darkness takes Sara by surprise. It causes her body to jolt and leaves her to dread whatever she will find in this seemingly endless void as she senses something she cannot quite describe. Despite the icy interjection and the nerves that bubble at the base of her stomach, Sara forces herself to press forward. Her eyes softly dart about the room, attempting to find whatever it is that Mr. Davenport would hide away from the work and this power she must acquire.

However, Sara only notices the dim lighting caused by the bed sheet covering the window. Sara finds this odd as Mr. Davenport could have easily attached proper blackout materials. She saw nothing except quality products in the warehouse. While Sara's body searches for the divine spirit of sorts, her mind stews on the obscurity of the window situation. Her head remains directed in the way of the bed covers, forcing Sara's leg to collide with the metal frame bed.

"Ow," Sara complains to herself.

Soft, slow movement instantly captures Sara's attention. Sara's eyes immediately fixate on the shadowy figure, causing her body to become ridged and her heart to pound harder than she knew possible. She expects something to follow this sudden sign of life. Whether it was an attack or something else is momentarily lost on Sara. Her fear has taken Sara prisoner. She is locked in her own body. She cannot do anything except watch as this form gradually proceeds toward her.

As slender fingers rest on Sara's injured skin, she is freed and can sense concern and compassion. It disarms Sara, allowing her shoulders to loosen and her breaths to normalize. Sara focuses on the hand that has begun to stroke her leg affectionately. Yet, while Sara has contained her fear, she still seems troubled by what lurks within this blackness as she gradually tries to pull away. However, the hand almost pulls Sara back before eventually allowing her to step away.

"Are you alright?" the soft, kind female voice asks.

Sara does not know what to think. She can barely breathe. Sara only watches as this figure hovers by her side. It does not appear to move. However, Sara knows this will not be for long. She is scared that this person will strike at her.

"W-what?" Sara sputters.

The shadowy figure inches closer to Sara and slowly reaches for her leg again, attempting to rid Sara of pain. Sara fights the urge to pull away as this set of fingers graze over where Sara had collided with the steel framing. They stay here, frozen. However, they know it will not last long.

"Your leg.... You're not hurt too badly?" the woman questions again.

Attempting to rid herself of this paralyzing confusion, Sara scans the room through the dim and barely navigational space before allowing herself to almost carelessly gaze down to where the woman's hand lovingly remains. Despite the metallic sink Sara spotted in the corner, the person's paw has what appears to be a thick layer of dirt and grime caked into the woman's skin. Although Sara's mind continues to search for a reason why the woman would be held here, seemingly living in filth, Sara ultimately finds her voice squeaking as she tries to answer this woman's query.

"Erm.... Yeah, I'm okay. I mean, it doesn't hurt anymore," Sara says through the unbearable tension in the darkness.

There is a pause. One that Sara can barely get herself through. Sara does not know what this person wants, and she cannot feel what they are experiencing. It does not sit well with her. Sara does not remember when she could not see into someone's emotional state.

"Good," the voice whispers.

All this standing about in the dark has begun to bother Sara, causing her to be vulnerable, fearing things beyond sight. As this woman's hand finally slips away from her, Sara's instincts take over. Without thought, Sara reaches out for the covers to the window and violently tugs it free. The sudden rush of light instantly burns both their eyes, although it harms the woman on the bed far more than Sara.

The woman's arm protects her aching eyes, leaving Sara to do nothing more than wait for the woman to settle and reveal her features to Sara. While Sara is more than aware that she has never met this woman, her long black hair, glowing blue eyes, prominent jawline, and cheekbones leave Sara staring. The woman is familiar to Sara, somehow already etched into her mind. As this odd sensation soon begins to fade, Sara notices the scratches and chaff marks encircling this woman's wrists. Then Sara finally comes to see that what she thought to be dirt under her fingernails had run up her hands to be dried, old blood.

Once the woman sees Sara inspecting her forearms, she defensively arranges herself so Sara cannot get a clear glimpse of the damage. In this moment of emotional quarrel, Sara senses something strange suddenly emanating from her. Something that causes Sara to step back. However, her feet fumble, causing her to trip. Her body jolts as she lands in a seated position. Despite the sudden rush of pain through Sara's spine, her eyes remain fixed on the woman.

"You-you're...." Sara tires. "Are you....? Are you who I think you are?"

While there appears to be much internal pain behind what Sara had asked on the woman's behalf, her expression still lifts into a warm smile. This small offering of kindness allows Sara to relax and see what she knows to be genuine emotion and body language from this bizarre and somehow accustomed person.

"And you're the one Charles went off to look for, are you not?" she asks in return.

As she cannot find a correct way to respond, Sara's bottom lip trembles and she cannot claim any control over it. However, this eventually subsides, allowing Sara to gather her thoughts and slowly maul through any viable answer. Unfortunately, nothing more than her immediate sputter seems to be coming to mind.

"How'd— I don't know how to...." Sara mumbles. "I'm sorry."

Although this almost extreme sight of Sara's frazzled state is somewhat off-putting, it does not appear to bother the woman Sara questions to be the Great Goddess. It only confirms what this woman believes and invites further conversation.

"So, you are," the woman has gathered. "Charles found you."

Sara does not know how to tell this woman anything. As Sara looks this woman in the eye, it is as if she cannot speak. It is like it is forbidden. Sara does not enjoy this sensation. It bothers her, and her stomach churns, feeling uncomfortable. Yet, this woman is still waiting for Sara to answer, wanting to know if Sara is the one. However, something tells Sara that this woman already knows.

"Well, yeah," she confirms.

The physical space dividing them is soon lost as the woman slowly slides off the edge of the bed and sits beside Sara, wanting to show the level of respect she already has herself. Despite Sara's hands on the freezing checkered steel-plated floor, the woman reaches out, softly pulling them free, and eventually takes hold of them. Caught off guard, Sara inadvertently holds her breath and stares at their suddenly intertwined hands in pure bewilderment and confusion. However, Sara eventually brings her line of sight back to the woman as sounds from the space below them uproar.

"Charles," Sara and the woman say simultaneously.

With her unexpected sense of danger returning, Sara pulls her hands out of the other woman's grasp and forces herself to stand. As the sounds continue, she rushes toward where she entered before noticing how they have begun to fade and cut off into pure silence. After a long moment of worry on Charles's behalf, Sara's mind gradually returns to the strange woman still calmly seated behind her. Sara turns, wondering if the woman is who she believes her to be. Questioning whether the power Sara intended to find has never left its source. And if the woman before her is the person who is both responsible for the trouble that has ravaged the world in recent days and the victim of extortion for her bestowed abilities.

"You're-You're— I mean, you're...." Sara attempts.

Another gentle smile makes its way to the woman's face. However, it is due to her sympathies for Sara, not because of any humor in that situation. Soon following Sara's lead, the long-haired woman stands and makes it to where Sara had come in, carefully standing beside her.

"I am you asking of.... I am the Goddess Charles would have mentioned to you," she cements. "And you are the one Charles went out to find, the one to hold the mantel— My mantel."

"Yeah," Sara agrees softly.

With the uncomfortable tension becoming unbearable, Sara and the Great Goddess pull their focus away from each other, knowing their presence is too much for the other. However, Sara notices the sudden rush of guilt and remorse that has come over the Great Goddess. This forces Sara to turn herself toward Mother Nature despite the growing anxiety that continues to take its toll. Sara sees the disappointment on the Great Goddess's shoulders.

"Hey," Sara says to gather her attention. "What happened anyway? Charles thought that you— We thought that you were no longer with us. And I thought they couldn't send the satellite without mimicking your abilities or with them...."

While Sara must strike up a conversation with the Great Goddess to ease the icy reception, another moment of further silence filled Sara with billowing fear. However, as this moment stretches out, Sara begins to assume that this must be due to thoughts from the Goddess's end. This seemingly endless and torturing time worries Sara about what might leave the Goddess's mouth. She dreads whatever nightmare can manipulate someone with such power and capability as the Great Goddess.

"I was taken from my home, my people, our temple and sacred ground.... I told Charles to find you. I thought I would lose my abilities. I thought they would rip them from me and focus them on their work. Strip the Earth from its natural protection," the Great Goddess begins. "I was wrong."

Sara is frightened to know the answer. However, she cannot help but ask, needing to know. She wants to understand what the Goddess has been through.

"What'd they do?" Sara asks.

"They suppressed my ability to access the powers that influence the atmosphere, tested my ability in use.... How they work and took samples...." Mother Nature begins to reveal. "They have successfully managed to recreate the full strength of the entity that I once could control...."

The seemingly pained breath between the Great Goddess's statements only reflects on Sara the deep-seated agony she faces in the wake of the experiments Mr. Davenport had subjected her to. The sight of this woman's emotional distress and the thoughts about what she would have endured leave Sara's attention to drift to her feet in shame.

"Sorry," Sara empathizes with her head down.

Sara and the Great Goddess uncomfortably return to their unnaturally silent state, allowing the unbearable tension between them to overwhelm them both. Their eyes softly drift about the room before they eventually find themselves locking onto the other's. As if this has somehow inexplicably granted them the strange ability to communicate with each other, their body movements appear to work in unison. With both of their eyebrows raised and their shoulders slowly begin to loosen. However, Sara's attention breaks due to the ever-growing call of the harbor. It distracts her from what powerful entities lie within the warehouse and the importance and weight of the mechanical beast that rests directly below them.

The Great Goddess watches Sara slowly pulse across the floor and eventually stops at the heavily rusted and barred window. The glass opening gives an excellent view of the street where Sara had been earlier with Charles. However, the street and what surrounds it are not the main focus in Sara's mind. Her thoughts are off in the distance, behind the disturbing sight of numerous warehouses and the odd building that blocks a percentage of the marina. Yet, Sara is grateful that she has this small glimpse of the waterfront and the cargo ship that rests within it.

"I need to go there," Sara states without understanding what she is saying.

While Sara would have instantly believed that someone would have deemed her insane for this unexplainable impulse, she is sure the Great Goddess will understand why she needs to go better than she can. As an answer to Sara's spontaneous claim, the Great Goddess comes over to the corroded window and stands beside Sara before looking out where the ship continues to act like some makeshift beckon.

"I feel it too – heavy – concentrated – power," the Goddess begins. "But not onboard.... It is as if it will lead us to it. Showing us what we need. Showing us what will unfold."

"I don't even know where it's going," Sara says as her words curl into a sigh.

The Great Goddess allowed her eyes to drift away from the waterline and slowly came to rest on Sara, wanting to tell her its destination. However, the Goddess also wants Sara to figure it out and control what makes them different from the majority. Into what it is that makes them eligible for god-ship.

"Yes. Yes, you do...." the Goddess suggests.

Sara finally breaks her serial stare into the strange beckoning of their possible future and soon rests her undivided attention on the woman. The expression of kindness and despair matched with whims of patience and what seems to be physical agony seeping from this woman, gradually extending to Sara. In this moment of brief torment, Sara realizes that the Goddess is merely an extension of the Earth itself. As this passing second of clarity comes to Sara, her mind slowly gathers from what the Great Goddess is trying to say. What it was the Earth needs to benefit from in this situation and how to achieve this goal.

"It's.... It's going to your station. Your ground...." Sara tries to explain despite the gaps in the knowledge surrounding how she gathers her information.

"Our temple," the Great Goddess says. "It amplifies my abilities.... It allows me to control the natural means of sustainability and order. But now, I wouldn't be able to alter as much as I once could after what Mr. Davenport has done to me."

Sara doubts what she is thinking. However, she still hopes that she is wrong and the Goddess may have a solution to the problem. It might make things easier for everyone. Yet, something tells Sara that she will see a lot of trouble at the Goddess's side.

"There's no way to correct it?" Sara questions.

The Goddess's chest almost sinks while appearing to simultaneously consider Sara's curiosity, though Sara's shoulders pull into herself in an act of defense. In a second, her trust in the Great One has vanished, replaced with a sudden rush of fear. A disturbing chill runs down between Sara's shoulder blades, and her stomach flips in expectation. It almost warns her of what is yet to come. However, all these warming signs soon subside like they were never there. It leaves Sara with a strange wave of almost nothingness and peace to wash over her. Bringing her back to the state she was a moment ago.

However, Sara still has a new constant worry in her mind. The fact that this wave of emotion had seemed to come from the Goddess herself. She fears that the Goddess may have the same empathetic ability as Sara. Sara does her best to think of Charles. She wonders if he has been hurt or has somehow managed to break free from the men within the building, hoping that dismissing her thoughts to a viable explanation would prevent something disastrous from happening. It appears to work for now as the Great Goddess's appearance softens and attention eventually retrains on the cargo ship posited out the window. It gives Sara freedom, allowing her to breathe and think.

"Power grows from one to the next, perhaps if you are the one Charles thought you to be.... I could pass my power on to you. You could correct the path the Earth is currently being lead down, instantly double the effectiveness of a single storm," the Great One proclaims.

While Sara had an inexplicable episode of terror, thinking that the Great Goddess would have something to gain from the situation, Sara only picks up on sincerity and hope emanating from her at this time. It slows the fear that Sara has of the woman. However, Sara is cautious, still unsure that the Great Goddess is the delight Charles believes her to be. Yet, Sara offers the Goddess the benefit of the doubt to ease the stress that wears them down.

"Well.... How—? How do we do that?" Sara questions reasonably.

As if knowing the answer already, Sara's eyes dart to the waterfront, where the oversized ship continues to call for her. The Goddess presses her hands against the glass, ignoring the sudden crashes that have begun to take place just below. Sara can only assume this to be the work of Charles as she is sure that it is Mr. Davenport's satellite taking the damage.

"Care to give me a hand?" the Great Goddess asks with her eyes lingering on Sara's.

It takes Sara longer than she would have thought to conclude what the Goddess asks. However, once she understands what the Goddess needs from this moment, Sara's hands reach up and rest beside the Great One's. As if they have done this before, their eyes close, and their breaths constrict as the air surrounding them drops below zero. The room soon begins to vibrate, rattling items within their immediate vicinity before a bright flash of light ultimately causes the glass before them and the thick bars to cascade out of its concrete socket. Sara's eyes slowly reopen to see their mutually created storm dissipate into thin air.

CHAPTER NINE

Sara finds herself fearing for Charles in this moment of extreme circumstances. She desperately hopes he will get away as he promised. Yet, Sara's focus is soon turned to the various debris, unevenly scattered at her feet, going on to spread out and over to the street. With Sara's attention on the road, she cannot help but notice how she and the Goddess would have a clear shot of the car while remaining hidden within a cavity built into the warehouse, hidden enough to avoid the unwanted sight of the armed men who survey the majority of the damage. However, these men soon bolt into the building, obviously realizing that the Great Goddess is the root of the problem.

"Alright.... Should we run for the car?" Sara questions despite knowing it is the only viable option.

The Great Goddess checks for the numerous armed men up through the window, knowing they will have no issue with capturing her or worse. As she finds no sign of these military men, the Goddess returns her line of sight to the stationary vehicle.

"To be honest with you, I do not enjoy that idea.... However, it does appear it will be our only choice," the Goddess agrees.

Sara notes the troubled tone within her voice and allows a troubled expression to flash across her face in light pity for the Goddess. However, their reservations about the plan get disregarded. Sara and the Goddess can hear the men above their heads. With this, they simultaneously allow their feet to propel them forward into a sprint.

Sara leads and eventually reaches the car a few seconds before the Great One herself. It lets Sara spot the guard staring at her through the destructive gap she had left behind. As this man appears to pull a gun from underneath his shirt, Sara's instincts take over. Rather than run as she would have thought, Sara raises an arm and smashes through the driver's side glass.

Despite the rocketing agony, she still finds herself grateful for the long, red-sleeved ensemble she had decided to wear today. Not only has it offered her at least minimal protection against the shards of glass and the cold breeze that seems to come with the Great Goddess, but it has also saved Sara from a rather nasty gash along her forearm on the climb down from the window. With the falling shards and the fact she must hurl herself into the car to open the door, Sara inadvertently rips a section of the fabric free from her shirt. Yet, it does not bother Sara in the slightest. She has successfully opened the door and has already managed to slide inside. She then reaches for the passenger side door, allowing the Goddess in.

"A bit dramatic, was it not?" the Great Goddess questions as she makes herself comfortable.

"Yeah. Sorry," Sara begins. "I saw a guy pull a gun and acted.... Little surprised you didn't have a little more of a reaction."

As she expected, the Goddess does not bother to reply to Sara's statement. Yet, Sara does not need one as she focuses on finding a spare key hidden inside. However, Sara slumps as she realizes Charles must have the only key. Sara releases a depressed sigh, alerting the Great Goddess to their situation. Momentary concern flickers behind the Goddess's eyes before retaining her more accustomed stone yet charming fashion. Once the Goddess settles with her calm demeanor, her hand slowly lifts toward the dashboard. Before Sara can question what the Goddess is up to, a bright spark of electricity lights the confined space. The crackling light extends from the Goddess's fingers as she touches the block before her. Although Sara is still shocked at the Goddess's ability to spark from her fingertips, she is left speechless as the Great One starts the engine. Sara can only stare in amazement before slowly allowing her hands to rise to the steering wheel. However, this thrilling moment is short-lived. Sara pulls her eyes away to the street only to notice the many guards that have started for the car.

"Thanks," Sara says.

As they are launched backward into the empty street behind them, the Great Goddess sucks in a deep breath. She is unhappy with their current predicament and means to accomplish what she believes must be done. However, she appears to contain her emotional and physical discomfort with the ride as they get jerked around while the vehicle spins, heading into the general area of the waterfront.

"Yes.... Well, we needed a means of transportation," the Goddess breathes.

Sara notices the Goddess's discomfort with the ride. However, she has chosen to disregard it as they are out of options. Sara also maintains their current speed through the relatively empty district streets. They must disappear before they must slow once entering the more busy areas of Washington anyway.

However, it had been quite some time without seeing anyone in a makeshift pursuit, and Sara found herself constantly checking behind them out of nerves. While there still appears to be no one trailing them, Sara's fear leaves her hand to tremble in expectation.

"You think they're behind us?" she eventually asks.

A slight silence occurs, although it is not as though it was unexpected. Sara is used to these silences when speaking to Charles or the Goddess. It has become almost second nature. Knowing that these two took their time to consider what they said, they cared about what came from their mouths. Like there is something important about the way they spoke to Sara. However, this moment fills with the graceful chiming of the Great Goddess.

"Of course," she answers. "They will be close.... They will also use every resource until we are within their grasp."

Although she knew this to be true in her own right, the cementation from the Goddess destroyed any hope Sara had before. Now panicked, Sara looks back as though Davenport's men would magically reveal themselves within the past few seconds. However, she soon finds the danger is lurking right in front of them as Sara's line of sight returns to the empty road ahead just seconds before two police vehicles simultaneously pull out. Their lights flash, blinding Sara for a beat, and sirens blaring louder than Sara thought they did. Perhaps it is because she knows this pursuit to be for her and not some distant thought in her mind, a danger she did not have to think about.

The police are slow enough to close the gap between them and Sara's. It sends a jolt of terror through Sara. As if knowing what Sara plans on doing in this time of alarm, the Goddess's hands come to level with the dashboard moments before Sara slams her feet onto the brake. Refusing to stop completely, Sara maintains a speed below the limit as she wishes the police were after someone before them. However, she knows they are for her and the Goddess beside her.

Although the initial slowing of the police vehicles did not have much effect in stopping Sara, another drop in speed occurred, leaving one of the cars to travel just behind theirs. They intend to trap Sara and the Goddess.

"What do we do?" Sara asks.

"We will not be able to outrun them.... Not like this," the Goddess realizes. "We will need to outsmart them," she claims as she gestures to a multilevel parking structure.

Sara's mind pauses, thinking through what the Great Goddess has suggested. Thinking the Goddess is correct and this might be one of their only options, Sara speeds up before their car does not have enough space to move and almost races through the slim entrance.

"They'll look for us in here," Sara ultimately states.

The Great Goddess fixes her eyes on Sara, noting the stress that threatens to consume her. "Yes, they will be."

Sara looks from the rows of cars to the Goddess, realizing what she means. Sara turns the wheel, aiming it for the ramp, thinking they will have better luck on an upper level. As they come to face yet another space filled with row after row of other vehicles, Sara slows as she attempts to find a way to avoid capture with the Goddess's unspoken suggestion. However, she receives more guidance to execute the Goddess's plans.

"Pull into a space and shut off the engine," the Great Goddess commands, knowing the police cars are not far behind.

As if without thought, Sara obeys the Goddess, pulling into the closest space available. They are tucked between a rusting van and an older model station wagon, leaving her to wonder who would have these vehicles in Washington. However, Sara soon brushes off this unnecessary thought and the overwhelming fear that continues to seep into her mind. However, the Goddess cannot help but notice how the engine still runs, possibly giving away their position.

"The engine," the Goddess says, tapping the dashboard.

"I can't," Sara replies.

The Great Goddess looks at Sara, unsure what she is trying to communicate.

"I don't have a key," Sara summarizes.

The Goddess quickly realizes what Sara said is true, leaving the Goddess to reach up and allow her eyes to close softly. Knowing that the Goddess is planning something, Sara instinctively inches away from the steering wheel as the Goddess suddenly strips the car of all charge. They both release a breath as if it had taken something from them. Yet, they seem to ignore the exhausting factor as one of the police cars slowly drives past. From Sara's advantage point, she can still see them from the driver's side and rearview mirror. Sara swears her heart, for a moment, does not beat. It ceases all rhythm, slowing her breath and leaving Sara to panic for her wellbeing. There is nothing more to do. Sara only watches as the car comes around again. Though, this time, they were sure to mute their sirens. Sara's eyes soon come to rest on the next ramp. They think they may have better luck with higher ground.

"Should we make a break for the next level?" Sara soon questions.

"No," the Goddess begins. "They have turned their sirens off. They are going by sound and visuals to find us. Turning the engine on will only cement our capture. Wait, they will believe we took the higher ground. We'll run then."

Sara cannot argue with the Goddess's logic. She can only hope it will be enough to avoid the hands of these men and make it to the waterfront. They fall silent as the police vehicle slows and gradually passes by. Yet before they can allow themselves to breathe, the car comes to a stop. No one steps out. However, the brake lights drive Sara mad. They taunt her and scream that she will get caught before finding what Sara knows she must.

"What are they doing?" Sara whispers.

"Waiting," the Goddess states.

As Sara ultimately believes this will be her end, the red glow of the police vehicle's rear disappears before the car finally heads up to the next floor. A long overdue breath exits Sara's mouth. It allows her to realize they do not have time to escape. Working simultaneously with the Goddess beside her, Sara reaches for the door and steps out. Both are conscious of leaving the door, wanting to avoid drawing unwanted attention to themselves.

"Harbor?" Sara breathes.

"Yes," the Goddess confirms.

They head for the nearest exit, wanting to leave this area behind them. However, both Sara and the Great Goddess pause. They sense something odd and out of place. Their eyes lift to where people should exit the structure, knowing someone is waiting for them. Sara turns, looking out the transaction windows, sure that it is safer than the exploded window she had already climbed from today. Noticing what Sara had, the Goddess heads off for the opening, knowing Sara will be close behind. Before they allow themselves a chance to think, they have already begun. However, Sara soon slows going on to bring concern from the Goddess.

"What is it?" the Goddess ultimately questions.

"You think we could have taken the ramp instead?" Sara asks as a serial afterthought.

The Goddess pauses, thinking over what Sara observed. Although, she soon pushes past this and continues on her way down. There is no going back now.

"No, they'll be waiting for us there," the Goddess states.

Without another word, they continue. However, Sara is conscious to watch out for other officers and any of the armed guards she has spotted at the warehouse. As she cannot see anyone worth noting waiting for them, Sara's line of sight occasionally falls toward the waterfront, memorizing every detail she possibly can. Time with Charles heightened Sara's ability to sense and empathize with those around her, the ground, and almost all living things. As they near the street below them, Sara finally notices how the Goddess's attention has been on her for quite some time.

"What is it, dear?" the Goddess questions.

"Not sure," Sara ultimately mutters.

Sara forcefully drags herself toward where she knows the harbor to lie and assumes that the Goddess will follow. However, she notes that the Great Goddess remains unmoving, her focus glued to Sara's skull. As if drilling into her mind, wanting to know what runs through it.

"What are you doing?" Sara ultimately asks, cautiously checking for overseers.

A long moment passes with no answer, no facial registration, only a long silence with her glowing blue eyes looking into Sara's. It causes distress and terror to inflame within Sara's chest, making it extremely painful for her to breathe.

"What are you waiting for?" Sara soon presses.

The Goddess stares for a beat longer, escalating the agony that Sara is experiencing. However, the slight pursing of the Goddess's lips eventually sooth Sara's worry and deep-seated anxiety.

"Tell me," Mother Nature finally demands.

"Tell you what?" Sara immediately asks.

Another brief silence takes place. While this time Sara is not physically pained as she was just moments ago, she still finds herself looking back up, wanting to know if the people attempting to surveil for them had indeed found them. Luckily, the space above them remains unattended as they had left it. It leaves Sara to focus on the Goddess, still awaiting her answer. Although, it does seem as though the Great Goddess has no current plans to enlighten Sara. The Great Goddess's face freezes, her shoulders remain tight, and her eyes focus on Sara's.

"We're going to get caught. You know that, right? Everything we're trying to accomplish will be for nothing if we are," Sara begins. "You want to return to your home, save everyone there, stabilize the planet or whatever.... We need to go."

"Yes. That will be correct. However, there is something else. Something on your mind. A conflict, one that is upsetting the course of what we're doing here. A conflict, splitting something within you. You are not even sure whether this is worth pursuing," the Goddess suspects. "If we are to do this, your mind must be clear and focused. Otherwise, all will be lost."

Sara cannot respond or close her mouth from pure surprise. It is locked open, shocked and taken aback. She wonders if this is what it is like for others to be around her as she uses her gifts. She wonders about the full extent of the Goddess's power and ability. What Sara will be able to accomplish once she acquires similar traits. Yet, she soon brushes this aside, not sure whether she should be thinking of such outcomes, whether Sara should be the next to have the power that this woman has surging through her veins. However, these thoughts disappear, and so does her amazement at the Goddess's display, leaving Sara to focus on what the Goddess had questioned.

"I guess I'm just wondering if I can trust you," Sara soon admits.

Sara would have expected some reaction, pleasant or otherwise. However, she is proven wrong as the Goddess seemingly maintains her composed state through all situations. It worries Sara. She does not know if she can trust someone who cannot show their fears.

"Smart," the Goddess eventually praises. "However, it is more a journey for yourself, is it not?"

"I-I— I'm sorry, I don't— What do you mean?" she asks.

The Goddess steps forward, gesturing to the water, knowing it causes Sara deep internal trouble. Their eyes linger here, waiting for the other to speak. However, Sara has nothing to say.

"This is not some naive journey to the Amazon as you may believe. It is your journey. Your entire life, the people that had surrounded you was scripted, molding you into what you must become," the Goddess claims. "You were always meant to be next in line for the role. The one that would help usher us into the new world."

Sara thinks of something fitting to say in response, something not profound but fitting. Although, to both their surprise, Sara does not respond to this extreme claim. She is strangely trying to find a way to digest what the Goddess has said. Sara tries to find a way to believe she is the one for the title of the Great One despite her insecurities and skepticism regarding the faith her father attempted to bestow upon her.

Once she riffles through her thoughts, Sara senses what the Goddess is experiencing. It cements what she had stated concerning what will come Sara's way. The only thing radiating from the Great Goddess is her deepest sincerity and kindness.

While one would think of this as comforting, it throws Sara off, screaming that something within these words will be worth regretting. However, there is something within herself that she has only felt occasionally. It compels her to believe at least a portion of what the Goddess has been feeding her. This familiar comfort leaves Sara to do nothing except walk to the waterfront with determination and acceptance resting high upon her shoulders.

CHAPTER TEN

Through the sudden low floating mist that has taken the harbor hostage, Sara can get past the intimidating security guards blocking the large vessel. While she can make out the shipping containers, machinery, and other items before her, Sara still struggles to see what is in front of her. As she carefully stalks across the busy deck, Sara soon thinks of the high probability that the Goddess has caused the fog to conceal their movements.

Although Sara cannot help but think of this blanket of clouds as a minor annoyance at this time. She had been able to practically run toward the cargo ship from the parking complex and through the many streets of Washington with this woman, determined to get to where she is now. However, the fog that has enveloped the deck distracts her from finding what is needed. Yet, this is not the only obstacle she faces in locating the desired.

However, Sara does not know where to find it, on board the ship or in the Amazon. Yet, she still knows there is something that she must encounter. As if informed of events before they unfolded. Something that she was not able to do before meeting Charles.

"Do you at least know where we're going?" Sara whispers, knowing the Goddess is behind her.

She is proven correct as the Goddess's hand reaches out and slides across Sara's forearm. It was the only answer that Sara required for the moment. More so since the hand swiftly guided her away from the small gathering of guards and to a more masked section of the deck. They find themselves tucked between two old and rusting shipping containers.

Once reaching a stop, Sara could not help but check to see that the coast was clear. Luckily for the two of them, the crew had seemingly not noticed Sara and the Goddess slip past them. It keeps them safe for the time being.

Sara allows herself to ease, dropping her tense posture, and gradually regulates her breathing before eventually noting the icy reception the Goddess gives her. It frightens Sara to see the Goddess like this. She does not know what to expect. However, Sara hopes the Goddess will keep herself calm.

"We are aboard a ship that Mr. Davenport has personally hired," the Goddess begins with hints of anger and irritation. "It would be best not to draw attention to us."

Sara heard the Goddess. However, something about how she said it scares and confuses Sara. It leaves her more nervous than she expected. Yet, Sara tries to move past this sensation. It does not appear to work.

"Draw attention?" Sara parrots.

Sara's eyebrows as she realizes the full magnitude of the Goddess's internal rage and what must have happened in the past to bring about such a strong reaction despite knowing more hides beneath. However, the only answer the Goddess permits herself to give is a reserved head nod seconds before allowing her attention to drift toward the line of restaurants and stores. She only stares at the long-abandoned stretch of the usually engulfed portion of Washington.

While silence from this woman is not unusual, how the Goddess is going about it is what frightens Sara. The softening of her features, a slight slump in her shoulders, and what appears to be sadness in the Goddess's eyes bring about immense discomfort on Sara's behalf.

Sara does not know how long she can ignore the sad and terrifying aspects of the Goddess. These traits weigh Sara down. She cannot deal with them much longer. However, this does not mean she does not care why the Great Goddess acts like this.

"What is it?" Sara asks. "What's wrong?"

Before finding the time to enlighten Sara about her emotional quarrel, the Great One thinks of the many actions that should happen shortly. Momentarily wondering whether or not things will play out as she believes they will. Sara will take the mantle of the Great Goddess and foil Mr. Davenport's plans before he can launch his satellite into orbit and allow the power to evacuate the impurities of the planet, resetting the Globe's overall condition. Although these thoughts seem to be in the same predictive manner as they were years ago, something is missing that leaves the Goddess in uncertainty. Something she did not think she would have difficulty foreseeing or sensing. However, she cannot predict the company and all the players involved in what is yet to come.

"I was hoping that Charles would be here," the Goddess stipulates.

Sara's face sinks, once again thinking of how they had abandoned him in Mr. Davenport's facility. She thinks of what they could do to him if they had captured him like Sara found herself believing. The thought instantly sends a ripple of depression through her, leaving Sara to follow the example of the Goddess. However, she has hope that Charles has escaped Davenport's grasp. Her eyes drift toward the pier, searching for any sign of Charles.

"I sent him to find you," the Goddess whispers. "I found him while he was still young.... Charles was in a difficult spot. He just left his job and everyone he knew behind. He was mentally unwell."

The sincerity in the Great One's voice and the sudden depth of Charles's past leave Sara's chest to deflate and her breaths to constrict in fear and anticipation. However, she cannot bring herself to look the Goddess in the eyes, not while she explains what Sara wishes to know. It is as if Sara was somehow ashamed despite the overwhelming need for the knowledge. While she had a general understanding of what Charles and the Goddess had planned, Sara does not know the plan for her, her future, and what transpired to create the dire situation between them and Mr. Davenport himself.

She must know the importance of the decisions made before their dramatic encounters. It determines what she will do next. However, something tells Sara she does not get much say.

"He quickly became one of my closest followers and believers.... He was always there and did as I instructed him," the Great Goddess says. "I saw his loyalty, it eventually led to him being my advisor of sorts.... And trusted partner."

The Goddess lifts her hand and creates a small ball of ice from individual ice crystals before letting this ball swirl above the palm of her hand. While Sara had been reserved and had not permitted herself to look at the woman, she could not help but rest her eyes on the revolving ball of ice. However, it is not due to being memorized as Sara would have been earlier. It is because she picks up on strange emotions as she watches the Goddess's fingers control the spin.

"I trusted him to know what is for this world, my part, and yours. It is why I knew that I could send him to find you. Charles wanted nothing more than to help achieve this great feat," the woman says softly. "I thought after all this.... he would be here."

As the Goddess had finally ceased speaking, Sara noticed the movement from behind one of the containers they used for concealment. She slowly drags herself over enough to get a glimpse of Mr. Davenport and a few of the men who chased after them at the warehouse. Rather than cower away from the advantage point and away from Mr. Davenport, Sara strangely remains seated. She wants to watch what they are doing aboard this ship. She cannot hear what Davenport is whispering to his adversaries, though she can see the damaged device getting loaded into the rusted hunk of metal she is leaning against.

She smiles, noticing it to be the one Charles had set out to destroy. Perhaps he had done what he had promised and escaped and halted Mr. Davenport's intentions by eliminating the machine. However, as the men load the oversized device into the container, Sara shudders from the vibrating of the cool steel as they do so. Yet, before she pulls away from this uncomfortable sensation, she notices a slumped figure getting escorted toward what Sara assumes to be the main control center. Without even seeing his face or any other identifying traits, Sara knew this man was Charles.

Once she realizes this, Sara permits herself to return to the more comfortable and hidden spot she was in a moment ago. Yet, it is not to hide away in fear. It is to gather her staggered breaths and to find the Goddess's eyes, hoping to bring her joy. However, the sudden chill that has overcome them alerts Sara to the Goddess's changed plans. At this moment, Sara shifts her body, needing to watch out for Mr. Davenport.

Yet, before Sara can get into position, they face something they both wish would not have to. Before Sara can turn, shivers run down her spine as she notes the manly shadow draped over them. She knows who is waiting for them.

"It was Sara, wasn't it?" Mr. Davenport asks, stepping in front of her. "I'm sorry. I'm not normally so rude. Your name just slipped my mind."

As Sara's heartbeat spikes, Mr. Davenport kneels before them. It brings him to near eye level with her. While he appears calm and collected, the nerves that Sara can pick up on tell her that he is rightfully fearful of the power the Goddess wields. More since the ice ball she had created has slowly been morphing into a defensive dagger, playfully gesturing to him.

"We won't need to use that, now, will we?" Davenport questions as he places a hand over the blade and presses it down.

His eyes dart to the Goddess, wanting to show how he can remain calm in the face of her attempts at intimidation. However, the Goddess does not waver or seem bothered by Mr. Davenport's almost fearless act. The only registration she allows herself to give is letting Davenport drop her blade.

"You, Mr. Davenport, are more than aware that I only strike when necessary and called for," the Goddess states. "Now, tell me, is it called for?"

The seemingly ever-burning stare between these two would be enough to cut through glass, cold and sharp. However, within the overbearing tension between Mr. Davenport and the Goddess, a wave of nausea unexpectedly washes over Sara. She turns away in a rush, leaving them to their deadly interactions, and forces herself to try to regulate her breath. As Sara slowly inhales and exhales, she can still hear the toxic exchange.

"Of course not," Davenport assures.

Although she had already drooped the icicle, the Goddess effortlessly cascaded the ice to the water with a simple flick. She is trying to show that she is willing to play nice. However, it does not seem convincing.

"Glad to hear it," she sarcastically proclaims.

With this, Mr. Davenport returns his focus to Sara, still awaiting her answer. However, he can see the state that she is in. It allows her to collect herself. As Sara still fights off this sudden and immense sickness that has taken over, she turns her head in their direction, knowing that they are there and waiting on her. Although, it sadly takes Sara a while to overcome this odd and crippling wave of nothingness and notice what Mr. Davenport is seeking.

While he had been kind enough to wait on her upon seeing her unwell condition, Sara soon sensed the impatience that emanated from Mr. Davenport and the Goddess. Sara's eyes softly rest on Mr. Davenport, feeling something else she cannot put her finger on. It is not an overbearing emotion or thought within the impatience of this situation. It is almost pleasant and leaves Sara to wonder why it would come from the man sent to destroy their plans. Despite this strange aroma seeping from him and many thoughts in his mind, Sara still manages to understand what he is after.

"Yes. It is Sara," she soon answers through the wall of distortion.

Her eyes soon become slant, narrowed with bewilderment toward Mr. Davenport. There is something about him that she does not understand. He is not the person she remembers from the bar.

"Sara.... That's a lovely name," Davenport humors. "I take it you're cold. After all, I'm cold. Would you like to take this trip inside?"

Sara cannot help but notice the sincerity in Mr. Davenport's voice and the overall impression he gives her. After a short moment lost in this seemingly honest offering, Sara eventually allows her eyes to trail across the obstructed deck to the control room. She soon wonders whether Mr. Davenport intends to gather them in the same room to make their theoretical demise, restrained to a singular and compact space. However, Sara realizes the numerous mistakes in this tactical plan, understanding that Mr. Davenport would never be this naïve or stupid, and soon realizes that he is telling the truth. Even if it might be for a hidden purpose that she does not fully understand yet.

"Yes," Sara finally accepts.

The side eye she receives from the Goddess causes Sara to look the other way, focusing on where she knows Charles is. As they all come to stand, Mr. Davenport directs Sara to a more secluded section of the ship. He takes her away from where she had seen Charles. However, not all seems lost as the Goddess gets escorted to the same control center. Sara hopes having Charles and the Goddess reunited will not be a complete and total failure. Perhaps there was more to come, more to endure before finishing what they had started.

"Where are we going?" Sara questions.

Mr. Davenport leads her to a seemingly quarantined area of the cargo ship, complete with a steel bolted door and guards waiting soundlessly outside. It frightens Sara. She does not know what he plans to do. Her mind tries to find a way out of this predicament and find Charles and the Goddess. However, Sara knows she must speak to Mr. Davenport.

"You'll see," Mr. Davenports states.

With this, the door opens from the inside. Somehow, someone knew that Davenport was waiting to enter without any movement or communication. It leaves Sara to curiously look up and notice the small camera staring down at them, watching them no matter how benign. Although they have stepped inside, Sara's mind is still on the camera, letting her know how they knew their whereabouts. It is from the lens' range and angle.

Yet, she eventually comes to brush off this unnecessary thought as the overwhelming yellow-tainted lighting engulfs the stretch of grated platforms and many staircases that run down the uniform lines. Sara cannot help but look over the railing and into what initially appears only to be an empty space below. However, Sara soon realizes her mistake.

"What is this?" she asks.

Mr. Davenport merely as he continues on his way, knowing that she will be tailing close behind. His feet quickly bounce down the stairs, allowing him to be amongst his workers as they transport the numerous parts for what Sara ultimately understands to be the atmosphere-altering satellite. The sickened sensation that Sara had overcome slowly makes a reappearance as she comes to realize that Charles had not succeeded in the destruction of the device. With no choice, Sara watches the men and women stride past with mostly smaller parts and organized chunks while the occasional large and identifiable pieces to the machine roll by in carts.

"So, what Charles did...." Sara tries. "You're.... You're showing me it was for nothing."

Mr. Davenport's eyes become full of life like someone had stroked a flame behind them, leaving him with a completely different appearance from the drunken mess she had first encountered at the hotel bar. The man before her is clean-shaven and energetic with a proud posture. However, something else is present, conflicting with this new man he has suddenly become. It is an emotion holding Mr. Davenport back enough to distract him from what is in front of him.

"No. That would be a horrible thing to do," Davenport affirms. "I brought you down here so we can chat without someone trying to influence you. I wanted to talk to you."

Sara's feet halt while her attention remains momentarily fixated on the discolored and stained floor. Without taking his eyes off the door located at the end of the corridor, Davenport stops. He knows his proceedings with this one will be difficult due to reservations and loyalties toward Charles and the Great Goddess. However, this does not appear to stop him. Mr. Davenport spins on the ball of his heel and soon stares directly at Sara. It causes her to lift her line of sight to his almost unnaturally green eyes.

"There's more to this than you know.... Whether you believe me or not— It won't matter. It will hopefully be enough for you to question what happens around you," he says. "You're more important to this than you realize."

CHAPTER ELEVEN

Although Sara is defensive around Mr. Davenport and reluctant to hear his excuses or worse. The tangible reasons for the trauma he has been unleashing for his benefit. She has still found herself sitting across from him, waiting to hear what exactly Mr. Davenport could have to say. They sit in his temporary office, decked out with a decent desk and a few frames she believes to be family photos. However, the most striking feature is the glass panel along the wall, allowing her to see the beastly satellite getting prepared.

"I wanted to see the progress in person," Mr. Davenport claims.

Sara stares, unable to do anything else. She is stuck. Her feet do not move, her breaths cease, and Sara cannot fix it. Luckily, Mr. Davenport understands and gives Sara time to recompose herself. She needs it. However, it appears that Sara slowly pulls free from this trance.

"Back at the warehouse—" Sara attempts.

"Was a model," Davenport says while he makes himself comfortable. "I knew that Charles would be joining us sooner or later.... The Goddess made that clear. But you— You were the unexpected variable."

The pause between them allows Sara to return her gaze to the many workers going at the hefty hunk of metal mess. They watch sparks fly through the air and slowly settle on the ground. As she notes how the workers assemble the large device, she is left to wonder how such a thing could possess any power with the likings of the Goddess. With the Goddess on her mind, Sara's internal focus turns to thinking of how she appeared tortured in Mr. Davenport's care.

"How could you do the things you did?" Sara asks, even surprising herself.

A long, deep breath escapes Davenport's nose, deflating his chest. He is taking a toll from this war. It leaves Sara to question what she believes. However, what she receives from Mr. Davenport now is enough to tell her that he is unaware of the traumatizing events that he and the Goddess had undergone.

"What things are you referring to, Miss....?" He questions with his hand coming to his eyes.

After this short moment of notable weakness on his part, he seems to reclaim the energetic state he was in before entering the office. His shoulders lift and become level, giving him the appearance of strength and confidence despite the agony Sara sees him bearing.

"Bornstein," Sara answers.

Mr. Davenport seems to savor her name. It is like it sits in the back of his mind, and Mr. Davenport is trying to recall it despite Sara knowing it is the opposite.

"Bornstein," Mr. Davenport parrots.

Sara can see past the overconfident and somewhat arrogant front that he gives off. Her growing ability allows her to see and feel through a series of painful emotions tied to his memories. It gives Sara the chance to realize a portion of what he's trying to sell to her is nothing more than the truth. Unfortunately, her position is not the most pleasant and welcoming, which has already had Mr. Davenport in a defensive state.

"Didn't you storm the Goddess's land?" she asks.

A quick and soft look from Mr. Davenport confirms this. However, his expression tells her that there is more. Sara was filled with shame. Yet, she does not understand why.

"Yes…. I did," Davenport admits. "Anything else? Anything you want to know at this point? Because the Goddess bends the truth in her favor and leaves things out. She uses everything in her power to have things go her way. I mean, I doubt that they've even filled you in on various subjects. Including what they plan on doing with you once you reach the Amazon."

More than a thousand questions come to mind. However, none can escape Sara's lips. She pauses with her mouth open, hoping that she will somehow spit them out. Yet, this moment does not come. Sara only thinks of the many things Charles has told her over the past few days, the emotions, reservations, and how he prioritized what he told her. She thinks of the numerous times she begged Charles for the slightest detail, of the riddles and the twisted words from the so-called Great Goddess. Sara wonders if the man before her is as terrible as she believes.

It's at this moment that the space above them seems to rumble. The unnatural shaking of the cabins above immediately triggers Sara's attention, leaving her to do nothing more than lift her head to the source of the sound. Mr. Davenport also tilts his head up toward the sound. However, his movement is slower, like he had expected it.

"Even now…." Mr. Davenport says, pulling something up on the monitor before him.

After an excruciating silence, he turns the screen toward Sara. It takes her a minute to realize what she is looking at. However, she soon sees Charles, a couple of armed guards, and the Goddess before another more powerful rumble overtakes the ship. It topples a few items off Mr. Davenport's desk and breaks one of the frames as Sara notices the workers struggling to remain fixed to ladders and railings.

Fear for the men in the next room fills her chest before the Goddess on the monitor screen captures her attention. The anger displayed by her, the terror and reservation written on Charles, draws Sara closer to the screen, wanting to know what happens next. However, all that appears on screen is the ultimate settling of the Goddess and relief on Charles's part. It leads to the relaxation of the space that surrounds them. It eventually allows Sara to slowly let go of Mr. Davenport's desk, fearing that the Goddess would cause the ship to tip.

"You trust this woman? You barely know her and the extent of what she plans on doing with you. Yet, you seem to trust her," Mr. Davenport points out.

Sara stares, searching for something to trust. However, she is still reeling from the quake she had witnessed the Goddess create. Sara then thinks of how they had blown out the window to Mr. Davenport's warehouse, thinking that maybe the Goddess has reasoning for the close call with the cargo ship. Though, there is not much that can convince her of this at this time. Especially as the Great One reunited with Charles, the man she had admitted to needing. Why would her first instinct be to capsize the ship after receiving what she seemingly wanted most?

Sara pushes past the probability of getting misled. However, Sara is still unsure where her loyalties should lie. Her attention slowly lifts, focusing on Mr. Davenport, realizing that while this man may have done terrible things, she does not know the context or the extent of what the Goddess plans.

Perhaps he does have reasoning behind the calculated decisions that he has made and will continue to do so. It leaves Sara to realize that Mr. Davenport may be the only person willing to tell her of the past of this rift. However, she finds herself reluctant, thinking that perhaps she was told the truth, as compartmentalized as it may be. Sara believes Mr. Davenport is not the enemy worth fearing. However, she knows the importance of their dire situation. She knows that she must try.

"Why do you hate them so much?" Sara eventually asks.

While Sara's voice seemed washed out and faded, the question still took Mr. Davenport aback. He slowly pulls his shoulders back and presses himself deeper into his chair. As if thinking that this would help him gather his thoughts and find a way to tell Sara about the past. While it is clear that Mr. Davenport is attempting to remain cool and calm in this situation, Sara can tell that this question hurts him more than she initially thought. Not from how he acts, which would have been Sara's first giveaway, but from the pain reflected behind his eyes. It's something Sara sees daily, something she must face every time she looks in a mirror. It's the pain she carries on for her father.

"Your father?" Sara softly questions, recalling the events in the bar and inadvertently thinking of her own.

The pained look in Mr. Davenport's eyes does not disappear. It only appears to deepen, leaving Sara to draw her conclusions. Sara's eyes slowly dip toward her feet, wanting nothing more than to distance herself from the agony she had brought Mr. Davenport and the pain she had brought for herself.

"Yes...." He finally comes to answer. "We have a few things in common. Don't we?"

Sara lets out a long, overdue breath as her eyes meet his again. She does not like that he is correct. However, it is something Sara must face.

"I guess we do," Sara admits with a weight on her chest.

The stiff and forced sensation between them returns. However, it seems Mr. Davenport is the first to try to break the uncomfortable tension. While Sara's eyes are on Mr. Davenport, her mind is elsewhere. It leaves Mr. Davenport to lean forward, gathering her full attention. Yet, he is still unsure how to go about things with Sara. He awkwardly stares at her with his mouth constantly forming and reforming, trying to do nothing except get a single word to her. Sara soon comes to pity him for this moment, watching Mr. Davenport struggle with the thought that he cannot say.

"What happened to him?" she asks, wanting to get answers and help Mr. Davenport out of the hole he fell into.

Mr. Davenport stares at Sara. He knows he must tell her. Yet, it does not stop a crippling agony from taking control of him. Fortunately, Mr. Davenport moves past this, ready to tell Sara why he distrusts the Goddess.

"Oh, well…. I think you should think of him as the previous version of Charles," Davenport begins with his eyes wide on thought. "He worked alongside the Goddess years ago…. Like him, Charles— I knew the Goddess as a child. Did you know that?"

This small offering leaves Sara to do nothing more than stare at his almost pleading eyes. Though he does not leave her enough room to find a way to respond, Davenport exhales and looks at the construction of the satellite. Staring at something within this busy scene, something trained on his mind.

"I grew up believing in the order that she convinced us to believe, that she convinced my father to believe," he goes on. "That's until I saw her firsthand causing the isolated earthquake in our hometown with my father in the epicenter. He knew what she was planning and killed him for it."

The horror suddenly embedded on Sara's face causes Mr. Davenport to ignore her. Especially as he does not wish to relive the pain. However, he still struggles before collecting himself and slowly allowing his sight to rest upon Sara's empathetic face.

"I mean it when I say I don't mean to hate someone. I do. But if I'm going to be honest with you— With myself, that's why I hate the *Great Goddess* as she likes. Just like you knew I did. That I do…." Mr. Davenport admits while unintentionally festering in an emotional state.

The sight of Mr. Davenport's pain, trauma, and anger leaves Sara uncomfortably tugging at her hands to distract herself from the seemingly infectious tender feelings that emanate from him. Although, this does not seem to have much effect. Not that Mr. Davenport is taking her problems with the topic into consideration. He opens his mouth with his mind trained on what he wants desperately to get out.

"But I want you to know that I don't hate Charles. I don't. Like my father, he follows the Goddess because of the love that she's infected him with. It makes him do things that he wouldn't normally do. I mean, she's convinced him that the deaths of our fellow men is a good thing," he explains. "Without her words influencing you right now, does that sound like a good thing to you?"

Sara pauses slightly, thinking of how the Goddess and Charles tried to explain how the regular and usually mild devastation was good. While Sara could agree that the world needs stabilization and the natural way of life would appear to be the best option, the deaths of many men, women, and children never sat well with her. It leaves her to hear the fairly reasonable side to Mr. Davenport's argument.

"No.... No, it doesn't," she answers.

"What I'm doing will balance the world.... Freeze the melting icecaps, bring rain where there is drought, and stop tornados from forming and destroying everything in their path," Mr. Davenport continues. "You've seen what the world is capable of these past few weeks.... That's nothing compared to what the Goddess will bring. And you're the missing piece to her plan. She needs you."

A seemingly overly dense breath leaves Sara's mouth as she can only think of how Mr. Davenport has solidified the importance of what the Goddess plans for her despite them having no idea of the specifics. However, this leaves Sara to comb over everything stated and suggested to her within the past few days. It causes an issue in Sara's mind.

"She wants to pass the power on to me.... She and Charles have said that directly to me— You're telling me the same thing. So, how would she plan on destroying everything? If I had the power, would she only try to convince me? Would she try to be like this supervising Goddess?" Sara asks, trying to think how the Goddess could intervene with the yet-to-be-bestowed abilities.

Mr. Davenport falls silent, unsure of the answer. However, he does appear to think this question through, wanting to either find a way to put her at ease or genuinely figure out the Goddess's plan. However, he does not seem to come to a full conclusion.

"I don't know," he answers honestly. "I believe my father knew the details of what she was planning.... Although I only remember a fraction of what she must be doing. I'm sorry. I wish I knew more. Not for me. But for you."

The disappointment plastered all over his face makes Sara want to distance herself. However, her attention soon comes to drift again. She settles on the satellite and the workers who assemble this mechanical marvel.

"What are you thinking?" Mr. Davenport asks, wanting to patch the slight gaps in their conversation.

Sara's eyes dart toward Davenport as she searches for a way to answer him. However, it is more than clear that she cannot find anything to say at this moment. She can only sit with her mouth seemingly stuck in an awkward open position, hoping that something will come out.

"Ah.... I don't know. I guess I'm still just wondering who to trust," she says with a fake smile, trying to hide the struggle she has raging within her. "And to be honest.... I'm still not sure that's you."

"Good," Mr. Davenport states plainly.

Sara finds herself put off by the bluntness of Mr. Davenport's statement. It almost forces her to close herself off and focus on what lies behind his words. Although, she cannot find a way to understand the meaning of what he had said.

"Why-why is that a good thing?" Sara asks.

"It means you'll be more inclined to do what you think is right.... You're not putting all your trust in one person other than yourself. You'll be vigilant," he explains. "If anything, when the Goddess takes you into her temple, you'll be looking out for yourself and what you believe. If I were a betting man, I'd say your definition of the right won't be the same as the *Great Goddess.*"

After a slight pause, Sara lifts a hand to her chin and sits with the weight of what he had just gone on to explain. She can see no issue with it other than they now both expect the Goddess to do something that will manipulate Sara into doing her bidding.

"Yeah.... I guess you're right," Sara says in agreement.

They allow themselves to fall back into the silence that engulfs the room and simultaneously turn their focus toward the glass. Or accurately, to what lies behind the glass. Sitting in this awkward situation brings them to an unspoken understanding despite the information gaps they seem to share.

"Anyway, I think I should get you back up to the Goddess," Davenport unexpectedly announces.

Sara shoots him a look of confusion, thinking this may be able to ask what runs through his seemingly complicated mind. As she knows Mr. Davenport does not share Sara's ability, she almost instantly wipes it from her expression.

"I thought you would want to keep us separated," Sara says.

"No," he disagrees. "The Goddess wants to give her power over to you.... To do that, she'll need you to be with her. She must pass the mantel on, and if it came down to choosing who to have that kind of Earth-bending abilities, it'd be you."

Sara allows this to sink in, staring at Mr. Davenport, knowing it is his honest opinion. It seems to fill them both with mixed feelings. It almost forces them to sit and wallow in them for a moment.

"So.... Let's go," Mr. Davenport says, hoping to put an end to their discussion.

However, they both appear to continue to let this socially awkward time between them go on for a minute longer before they ultimately come to stand and make their way to the door. With another look at the satellite behind her and her final determination, Sara soon allows herself to press on and leave the space with Mr. Davenport accompanying her.

CHAPTER TWELVE

The walk back through the ship with Mr. Davenport by her side is harder on Sara than she would have realized. Dread builds with each step toward the Goddess. However, it is not because of the uncomfortable situation that will come their way, as one might believe. Sara wonders whether or not Mr. Davenport can feel the light pulsing in the ground that appears to harden as they close in on the command center. Yet, as they press on, Sara becomes more sure she is the only one experiencing the almost miniaturized quakes. Not that it makes a difference either way. Whether or not the ground beneath her feet vibrates in what seems to be expectance, she must confront the Goddess.

"Are you alright?" Mr. Davenport suddenly asks, noting Sara's ill appearance.

She looks at him, wondering if he cares about what will happen next or if he is the hidden agenda type. However, he does raise a few good points regarding the Goddess and her adversary, Charles. The truths are bent and stowed away to be used as bargaining chips later. Sara lets these thoughts go, thinking it would be better to relax. Yet, it does not appear to work.

The almost rhythmic vibrating trills with the industrial-like steal floors leave her sick in the stomach. Yet, moving forward and looking at what lies ahead of her only seems to matter worse. However, she must push past the overbearing sensation for everyone's sake.

"I don't think I like boats," she eventually replies.

Mr. Davenport smiles, knowing why. However, he does not keep it there for long. He does not want to offend Sara or make her think he is laughing at her. Sara needs someone, and Davenport knows it cannot be Charles or the Goddess.

"Oh," he says. "Well, the journey won't take long."

Sara stops shuffling for a beat to take a serious look at Mr. Davenport, giving her momentarily relief from the sickening pulses. Once he realizes Sara has stopped, he halts and returns the same gaze-curious expression. She does not believe him.

"It won't take too long?" Sara parrots. "The trip from the Washington harbor to the Amazon.... Won't take too long?"

"No. No, it won't," Mr. Davenport assures.

Sara does not move. She stares at Mr. Davenport with her breaths slowing as she attempts to figure out what he means. However, this will not be happening. Her eyes rest on him, hoping he will elaborate more. Yet, he only holds eye contact.

"Do you maybe want to explain?" Sara asks.

Her raising her eyebrows and how she lightly leans towards him causes Mr. Davenport to smirk at her confusion. Although he knows he should not find this humorous, he cannot help himself. Not at Sara necessarily, but more at the curiosity on her behalf, Mr. Davenport is more inclined to see himself in her position. He is always disoriented and never knows the full extent of what happens around him.

"Yes.... Well. You see, that's where physics comes into play. We use a technique we came across many years ago," he begins. "Let's see.... Have you ever heard of warps in time and space?"

Sara is confused. Mr. Davenport, Charles, and The Great Goddess have tried to convince Sara of the mystical world and everything it entails. She did not think Mr. Davenport would bring elements of science fiction into the mix.

"Isn't that theoretical?" Sara questions.

"It was until it wasn't…. Many have come across it over the years. Purely by accident, and we thought that something biblical or extraterrestrial had intervened. Or that it proved the existence of the divine," he says, trying to hide the smile that threatens to return. "While we both know that there is…. The divine had no part. It was science, time warps. It allows us to enter at a certain time and arrive at our destination sooner than we should have been able to."

Sara's eyes pull away as her head nods softly, fighting the nausea that continues to run her down. Through the sickness, she understands at least a small percentage of what Mr. Davenport was trying to explain. Luckily, Sara knew enough about what he was talking about to understand the full extent of the information.

Despite only spending a brief amount of time together, Sara is glad that her first impression of him does not appear to be more than a sudden surge of emotional quarrels. That his night in the bar was nothing more than the unsettled internal drama that undoubtedly rages within him. Even if she were to be proven wrong about him, Sara was glad to see who the man was. She knows in her core that Mr. Davenport is partially reasonable.

She eventually lets this go, knowing that this moment between them has already slipped away. As Sara and Mr. Davenport allow their gaze to drift from the other, they shuffle toward where they know the Goddess to be. Once they step on the deck, Sara's eyes instinctively cast out to the water. She immediately notices that they are not at the vacant harbor. After a quick scan of what surrounds them, or more accurately, not, Sara realizes that they have left Washington behind.

"Guess we're already on our way," Sara mutters half to herself.

While she spoke to herself, Mr. Davenport had heard, causing his face to sink. However, he almost forces his shoulders to remain firm and in place, as he attempts to reclaim his almost ever-changing calm and collected essence. It leaves him with the same strong appearance he wanted present for his conversation with Sara.

"I'm sorry about the lack of warning.... Timing is— Well, time will run out if we let it," he excuses.

A long, dense breath escapes her mouth. She does not enjoy constantly holding her breath in surprise. However, Sara knows it will not stop anytime soon. There is more to come, and it undoubtedly brings shocks.

"Yeah," she says as she notes the Goddess's figure within the cabin ahead. "I get the feeling."

Realizing the hesitation on Sara's behalf, Mr. Davenport kindly places his hand on her upper back, softly beginning to usher her in the Goddess's general direction. Once they both regain their pace, he allows his hand to drop back down to his side and head to dip, knowing that the Goddess watches on. As they reach the door to the cabin, Davenport cannot help but stop just short, allowing Sara to step in front. He uses her as a barrier between himself and the Great Goddess. However, this does not seem to do much as the Goddess's eyes instantly dagger into his.

"You two were gone for quite some time," the Goddess analyses.

Through the hate that emanates from the Goddess, Sara finds that it would be best to ignore this statement for a moment and sit across from the overanxious Charles. Although she feels almost betrayed by this man, she knows he needs support. There seems to be something off about how he acts around the Goddess. Sara cannot help but find this extremely odd as the Goddess was the one he was searching for all this time, with the heartbreaking thought that she may have died. While Sara finds herself confused by the fact that Charles seems to be emanating dread with the Goddess present, she notices how he allows his eyes to flicker between her and the floor. It leaves her filled with many thoughts and a swell of her emotions.

"You alright?" Sara asks Charles regardless of the disapproval.

As an answer, Charles allows his line of sight to trail up to Sara's face and fixates on her eyes. He forces himself not to break it as he has been doing since she entered the room. At this moment, Sara is more fearful than she would have thought possible. It does not seem like him, not the Charles she knows.

"Of course," he states.

Although his words are benign, Sara hears the understated pled behind them and notes how the Great One stares at them. Sara thinks whatever the Goddess had done on the monitor screen must have scared Charles into line. It causes Sara to try and devise a way to understand what had happened while she was with Mr. Davenport.

"We were just discussing what it would be like once I receive the mantel of Goddess," Sara finally comes to answer, knowing that this is what the Goddess seeks from her.

The pause in the Goddess's reaction leaves terror to bubble within Sara's chest. However, the woman soon allows her head to move in an agonizingly slow nod and her lips to part, giving Sara a moment to breathe. Sara does not know what she would have done if the Goddess behaved differently.

"Oh?" the Goddess puffs.

However, it does not appear that Sara wishes to give this information away. It causes the Goddess to firmly rest her eyes on Sara as if trying to persuade her to reveal the events beyond the guarded doors. Yet, Sara merely turns her attention away, facing Charles and the distant-minded Mr. Davenport. This act immediately enrages the Goddess and brings the miniaturized quakes back to Sara's attention. As the pulsing continues, she looks to the Great One for answers to the unnatural event. However, the Goddess does not notice that she causes this occurrence. Nor does she appear to note that it happens at all. It leaves Sara to question what is transpiring. Although, she does not get long to stew on the unsettling vibration.

"It must have been quite the conversation," the Goddess presses.

Sara struggles for a breath and to look into the Goddess's eyes as the thought of the rhythmic pounding continues. It scares her. Sara wonders if it is natural or if she should worry that she is having a medical episode. However, it still does not frighten her more than the Goddess. The Great Goddess has a powerful hold over her.

"Ah.... not really," Sara replies.

The uncomfortable tension within the space around them begins to slowly gather Mr. Davenport's full attention, leaving him to quietly signal for the guards he has stationed within the room and eventually exit without another word. However, he and Sara briefly lock eyes before he makes his way through the door, almost exchanging words with a simple glance. Yet, once Mr. Davenport and his men have left, it forces Sara to train her focus on the Goddess despite the overwhelming rage emanating from her being and the fear on Charles's behalf. Yet, it does not appear to be much more than the uncomfortable knot within Sara's chest.

"Anything worth noting?" the Great Goddess asks.

"No.... He just tried to convince me that the satellite was the best decision and it would save lives," Sara attempts to brush off.

Knowing what the Goddess is capable of, Sara does her best to think of things that would hopefully excuse the emotional state she finds herself in. However, she cannot help but fear that the woman before her will ultimately see past the charade that Sara is trying to pull off. The Goddess does not allow her eyes to unlock from Sara's. The Goddess's shoulders remain tightly wound. and her jawline firmly locked, giving the woman an overly aggravated appearance.

Although Sara must sit through this uncomfortable situation with the Goddess's intimidating presence wearing her down, she allows herself to turn toward the fading expression written on Charles's face. She wonders what could be causing the undeniable agony he must be going through, whether the Goddess is the reason behind it. Yet, the sudden realization on Charles's behalf forces him to close himself off physically and somehow mentally.

Sara almost jolts. She did not know that Charles was capable of such a feat. She did not know that anyone was capable of evading her abilities. It leads to Sara disconnecting herself from the situation at hand. Sara's shoulders pull forward, her head dips toward her lap, and her hands fold into the other. She sits quietly, knowing Charles and the Goddess are staring at her. While her mind deals with the swell of thoughts threatening to consume her, Sara lets herself momentarily relax. Although, it is interrupted.

Though Sara is in something that she could have never imagined a few days earlier, something that could potentially lead to her untimely death or unimaginable greatness, in this moment of unbearable mental distress, she realizes that this must happen. These events will climax and lead to something almost unearthly and unpredictable despite the warning she and everyone else receive. Realizing that this sudden rush of thoughts and unsteady emotions are not her own, Sara's head tilts toward the Goddess, thinking it may have originated from her.

However, she sees that this is not the case. It leaves Sara to conclude that it must have been Charles as his heart spikes, hands excessively sweat, and unrecognizable attributes overrun Sara's mind and body. Just as fast as the emotions had invaded Sara's being, they left without notice, as if Charles feared the Goddess learning the truth. Although, the Goddess does not seem to pick up on the abrupt rush of thoughts. It gives Sara the impression that he had only permitted her to know.

"And what do you believe the best decision is?" the Great One deeply questions. "Do you agree with him?"

Although Sara finds herself in a mental and emotional whirlwind, this question instantly brings her back to reality. Yet, there is a moment where Sara becomes lost in this thought. It leaves her to do nothing more than stare at the Goddess. It gives the Goddess reason to believe there is more to consider than what Sara had stated and what must be said.

"Balance," Sara soon comes to answer.

While Sara attempts to deflect the Goddess's skepticism, she knows she must have inadvertently triggered it. If not before, she has now. The Goddess's head lifts in disbelief. However, the Goddess soon allows her posture to relax and overall intensity to subside.

"So.... What now?" Sara dreads to ask.

The Goddess and Charles focus on Sara despite the softness she had tried to induce, forcing a shot of nerves through her stomach. Although, the uneasy sensation fades as she notices Charles's familiar sympathetic expression. While Sara knows Charles sides with the Goddess, she also knows he will still look out for her. As long as he is here, Sara is somewhat safe.

"Who would we be to give up a free ride?" Charles asks mockingly. "Besides, we think it would be best to keep an eye on Mr. Davenport.... We can't afford to have him beat us to the punch."

"Makes sense," Sara notes.

While this did not instantly appear to be anything worth analyzing, the Goddess's attention flickers between them, like this had confirmed something to her. Sara questions what was said to trigger this response from the Goddess. After a long moment, Sara realizes that she and Charles have acknowledged that Mr. Davenport can still intervene with their current plans. She realizes that the Goddess must have found out about another satellite and is not speaking theoretically.

"Yes.... We will make the journey, then we will end this once and for all," the Goddess states.

"End it?" Sara cannot help but ask.

The pause in the Goddess's eyes leaves Sara to cross her arms in defense and look to Charles, hoping for some guidance in this situation. However, it does not appear as though he will be of any help at this time. He faces the nearest window as if trying to gauge where they are or perhaps trying to stay out of the uncomfortable conversation. It does seem more likely, given the situation.

"To bring balance to our world," The Great Goddess clarifies. "It is what you want, is it not?"

While Sara wanted to answer the Goddess, she paused, unable to get words out. Luckily, the Goddess has similar thoughts, questioning what they are doing. It gives Sara enough time to recompose herself.

"Yes," Sara answers.

As the tension between Sara and the Goddess seems to pick up and become a little heated, they turn their attention toward Charles. Despite the usually cold and almost distant emotional reservation from the Goddess and the lost state Sara usually found herself in, their expressions appear frightened. It is as if Charles had suddenly informed them of something alarming.

"Charles?" Sara softly whispers.

While they all appear frightened, it seems Charles is the only one who knows the reason for the sudden shift in their environment despite the women's empathetic abilities. Although, it does not take long for Sara and the Goddess to realize why Charles gets burdened with such crippling fear.

They step forward to the window where Charles has lost himself. The dark hanging cloud, clearly rough seas, and sparks of electricity leave Sara and Charles to turn their gaze to the Goddess. However, the expression on her face is enough to tell them that she is not the reason behind this horror. It makes an instant fear wash over Sara before her thoughts get abandoned, almost forcing her to run for the door. Without even checking behind her, Sara knows Charles and the Goddess are following not far behind.

"Come on," Sara tries to encourage.

Although they make their way across the open deck, Sara cannot help but slow before coming to a brief stop as she reaches the guarded door where Mr. Davenport had revealed so much to her. She momentarily wonders if they will grant them access inside, though it seems as though the guards and whoever watches on from the monitor are expecting them to show up at any second. A sigh of relief is quickly shared between Sara and Charles as the door suddenly swings open, allowing them to enter.

CHAPTER THIRTEEN

The flickering lights within the enclosed hallway fill Sara's chest with fear. She pauses, wondering if the vessel could endure such an enormous and powerful storm. Seeing the overly concerned expression on Charles's front is enough to tell Sara that he is just as terrified as she is. However, the falsely calm demeanor that the Goddess almost forces upon them makes Sara's face sink and her shoulders slump. It immediately enraged Sara, which caused her to turn and bounce down the nearest staircase, wanting to get far away from the Great One.

"We'll be safer down here," Sara tries to excuse with exhaustion.

Charles swiftly pounces by Sara's side. Perhaps he thinks he will be more likely to survive the trip to the Amazon with Sara. Or he believes that she will be safer with him. Either way, Sara does not seem to mind. She genuinely enjoys his company despite his ongoing legion with the Goddess. However, Sara does believe that Mr. Davenport is correct in his observation. Charles follows her with a blind and mediocre understanding. It leaves Sara with some hope for him in what appears to be only a dark circumstance.

"Was it true?" Charles soon whispers with his attention faced elsewhere, trying to hide the fact that he is speaking to her.

Knowing the danger they both potentially face, Sara briefly looks over her shoulder to the Goddess to see the bitter and distant expression that extends to all who acknowledge her. Hoping they will provide the Goddess with enough distraction, Sara returns her focus to the space ahead, following suit and trying not to look at Charles directly.

"Was what true?" she questions.

The momentary silence on his behalf causes Sara to quickly glance at him, wanting to see if he had registered her inquiry. However, she soon realizes this to be a slight mistake as the Goddess's focus lightly grazes over them. Luckily, she soon loses interest, leaving Sara and Charles to resume their concealed conversation.

"What you said about Mr. Davenport," he finally comes to clarify. "Was it true?"

Sara waits before answering. She wants to know why Charles asks if it is for the Goddess' benefit or his curiosity. Once Sara realizes why Charles must understand, she relaxes.

"More or less," Sara answers.

While she feels a connection with this man, a man who has Sara wishing for the best possible scenario where he is in the dark about the Goddess's plans, Sara still does not know whether or not he is worth trusting. It leaves her to regret having to keep him at arm's length. Yet, she must now more than ever to do so.

"He mentioned his father, didn't he?" Charles carefully asks, not wanting to appear as desperate to know the extent of the events that unfolded between Sara and Mr. Davenport as he truly is.

Without considering the Goddess behind them, Sara fixates on Charles. She holds this eye contact, thinking through her impending response. However, she cannot think of a way out of her predicament and eventually believes that partial honesty will be enough to free her from the constant pestering.

"Yes," she finally confirms.

An awkward moment passes. Sara does not know how to respond. However, Charles still wants more. He must know. It affects everyone and what will happen next.

"What else?" he continues to press.

Not knowing how to continue, Sara slowly pulls away physically and walks closer to the steel walls while she tries to control her breathing. As she wonders how she will follow through with their plans, her eyes lift, noting Mr. Davenport waiting for them at the end of the corridor.

"I see that you noticed the storm," he states with a strange smile resting on his slightly corked jawline.

"Ha," Sara blurts sarcastically. "Yeah, we noticed a bit of drizzle ahead."

The banter between these two instantly sends a flush of irritation into the Goddess's face. It causes what almost appears to be a burn mark to manifest on her otherwise perfect mug. However, the momentary lightness from these quips is soon drawn to an abrupt end as the visible anger on the Goddess's behalf immediately captures everyone's attention and triggers a fair amount of terror.

"You should come with me then," Mr. Davenport says as he leads them away from his precious cargo.

Sara cannot help but speed up, hoping to distance herself from Charles and the Goddess. As she reaches Mr. Davenport's side, they exchange another look as if telling one another of the danger that may unfold. Yet, their almost telekinetic communication stops as they both feel the sudden rush of cold air brush down their spines. They lift their heads and quickly examine the ceiling above them. However, they cannot find anything that would explain the icy shudder that they experienced. Soon realizing that the Goddess must have been the cause, they slowly turn to face her, wondering what she has to say.

"What have you done?" the Great One questions sternly.

Mr. Davenport is confused. He wishes that the Goddess would be more enlightening. Yet, Mr. Davenport sadly must indulge the Goddess.

"What do you mean?" Mr. Davenport asks as he brings a hand to gesture in the air.

How he had responded causes Charles to take a step between him and the Goddess, clearly wanting the following conversation to be civil. However, he gets waved off by the Great Goddess. Charles's chest deflates in disappointment, and his eyes lower to the ground as he slowly returns to his benign position. Not that Sara could blame him for trying. She knows of the danger that could unfold before them.

"The storm," she strangely answers in short. "You now have the capability, do you not?"

"Heh.... Well, that's not my doing, Dame Nature," Mr. Davenport begins.

Hesitation and bewilderment wash over everyone. They do not understand what Mr. Davenport has said. Even Sara expected that this storm had something to do with Mr. Davenport. However, he says otherwise.

"Have you not come across it in your time? The Devine portal, otherwise known as a time warp?" Davenport continues.

Sara's eyebrows frown as she notices how Mr. Davenport has spoken to the Goddess. It is as if he is telling her something else beneath this statement. She turns to the Goddess only to see how her expression has become blank. However, the Goddess soon resumes her customary confident and calm appearance before the cold sting of her vengeful state regains strength.

"It can often present itself in the form of a storm.... Other times— Well, things can get a little trippy. Especially out here on the ocean." Mr. Davenport continues.

Everyone falls silent for a beat as if they had ceased to breathe. Their focus is on the Goddess. They want to see what she will do next. They want to know if she will continue to speak with Mr. Davenport before making her way to the Amazon jungle. Or if things will get a little more complicated and end in disaster for everyone aboard.

However, before the Goddess could reply, she contained her inner beliefs and impulses and then turned her line of sight to Sara. The Goddess stares at Sara as though trying to read her thoughts or figure out her opinion in this torn situation. However, Sara's blank expression and worn-down attitude make things difficult for the Goddess. It interferes with her ability to empathize with Sara. It causes the woman to pull her head back as she soon realizes the full extent of Sara's disbelief in her mission and the political placement she has taken.

Appearing to have calmed herself, those surrounding them resume their designated workload. While Mr. Davenport and Sara remain planted where they stand, Davenport firmly holds eye contact with her as if questioning what she plans to do next. Yet, the momentary silence does not seem to bother any of them. It merely gives them enough time to breathe in this tense situation. Yet, their peaceful break finishes as Sara watches the Goddess disgracefully falter as she tries to answer Mr. Davenport. However, while the Goddess continues in an attempt to solidify a response, Sara is thrown by the brief insight into the Goddess's state.

An overwhelming sense of pain, confusion, and an unhealthy amount of regret and anger suddenly invades Sara's well-being, leaving her to sway from the agony of these toxic qualities. While it only took a moment to receive this flush of hateful and almost remorseful information, Sara stews on it for a long beat as she struggles to understand these strangely specific yet vague thoughts and emotions that emanate from the Goddess. Although, Sara gets the sense that the Goddess is just as lost in this moment as she is, caught in a struggle.

"Yes.... Yes," the Great One is eventually able to spit out. "I've heard of it from time to time."

The Great One's face slowly softens like when she first encountered Sara at Mr. Davenport's warehouse. The warm, seemingly friendly, and oddly familiar woman causes Sara a deep discomfort, leaving her to slowly breathe out, dealing with the sudden sickness in her stomach.

However, it does not appear to make much of a difference as the pain and nausea rage inside her. Especially as she soon becomes the Goddess's focus.

"Have you?" she softly questions.

It takes Sara a moment to realize what the Goddess truly means. However, once she does, her face flashes in pure realization, and the wave of nausea she has been experiencing slows alongside her breaths. The Goddess's head lifts with her deepest sympathies while watching Sara struggle with something the Goddess has endured for many years. Struggle with something that she does not understand, nor does Sara know how to control and keep at bay.

"A little," Sara almost whispers, feeling the now forced chemistry between herself and the Goddess.

While she and the Goddess had been strange with each other when they had first encountered one another, Sara grew to appreciate the company the woman gave as well as the deep-seated respect that she had for the woman capable of such mind-bending feats. Sara wishes that she could revert certain things to how they were before the world started to fall apart and that she could trust the things and people around her. Trust her ability without ruining what is best for the world. Although, she knows it is useless to think this way. Sara knows she must move forward, sacrifice what she has ever had, and give herself to the world.

Despite what runs through Sara's mind, everyone else around her appears to cave under the pressure of this intense interaction. Their chests inflate before they seem to crumple from the goddess' presence before their expressions droop, and general energy eventually drains as though it had taken everything out of them simply being in the same vicinity as one another. As Sara attempts to overcome the same sensation, thinking of a way to continue that would hopefully benefit everyone for the time being. She notices how the Goddess glances at

Mr. Davenport. It's almost kind. Yet, there appears to be something else present that leaves Sara with the impression that there is much more to what is unfolding than she knows.

"Where are we going?" the Goddess finally asks Mr. Davenport.

However, like Sara, it takes him a moment to realize that the Goddess is speaking to him. Yet, his eyes widen once he does. He is surprised by how she has approached him on the matter. Though his eyes gently glaze over Sara as he soon comes to believe that the Goddess must be doing this more for her benefit than anyone else's.

"We're just going to bunker down in one of the ship's cavities," he answers like it means nothing.

He turns and walks toward where he intends to place them for the time being as they ride out the nightmare-worthy storm. However, none of them seem enthused by this idea. As Mr. Davenport reaches the slim, dimly lit room, he pivots to see that Sara, Charles, and the Goddess only stare after him. Yet, Mr. Davenport remains planted there, staring back at them before realizing he cannot convince them to patiently wait out the storm in such a cramped and unwelcoming space anytime soon. Mr. Davenport releases a long, overdue breath, and his shoulders cave forward. It almost propels him back toward Sara and the others while what appears to be a troubling thought on his mind.

"Alright.... I think I know what you want," he states. "Follow me."

As Mr. Davenport presses on, gliding directly past them, Sara realizes where he has begun to lead them. Her face instantly pulls back in shock, and her breaths constrict as she watches the Goddess edging closer and closer to where Sara knows the satellite to be. Mr. Davenport knows the struggle that Sara is sure to be facing and instinctively checks over his shoulder to Sara. He wants to know how she is dealing with the troubling thoughts that must be overwhelming at this very moment. However, Mr. Davenport faces more as his attention diverts to one of his men.

"Sir?" the guard reasonably questions.

All their focus momentarily lies on this one man, waiting to be cleared. However, Mr. Davenport is the only one who remains neutral and waves everyone through. Yet, Sara cannot help but notice how Charles seems curious before slowly turning her attention to the Great One.

She watches as the Goddess's expression curls in a twisted way. Although, Sara is not all that surprised. However, there appears to be something else within the sickened glimpse of happiness and rage. She seems to fight something within herself, filling Sara with terror and a sliver of hope.

"It's alright.... Let us through," Mr. Davenport assures the guard.

With another look of concern from the armed man, he reaches across and opens the wideset door, letting them see the almost completed work. Sara and Charles recognize the piece of machinery instantly. Although, this is the Goddess's first time seeing the mechanical beast. She takes her time to comprehend the sight before her. Leaving everyone to watch as the Goddess gradually steps forward with her brow high and reaches a hand up to the cool steel as if feeling the pure power the device is capable of.

"You have done it," the Goddess almost whispers to Mr. Davenport.

While the Goddess and Mr. Davenport's eyes awkwardly meet, the Great One's hand suddenly drops, and posture corrects as though something had clicked within her mind. As if the device has merely cemented a portion of what she counts on unfolding, of something that the Goddess knows is sure to happen in due time. With her head still riding high, she pulls herself away from Mr. Davenport's immediate reach and begins to walk parallel to the machine, both sensing and knowing the potential this satellite holds. Although there is much that the Goddess is grateful for in this machine, the thought of what Mr. Davenport plans on using this device and Sara for leaves the Goddess to stew on her bitter hatred. While the Great Goddess continues to think of how Mr. Davenport can and will use them to his advantage, posited against the Goddess, she slows enough to allow him a chance to approach her.

"Yes.... Yes, I have," Mr. Davenport eventually acknowledges with his eye trained on his accomplishment.

Sara's pulse quickens, believing that the Goddess may destroy any chance Mr. Davenport has at succeeding in his effort by devastating the advanced contraption before them. As if they could read her thoughts, Charles and the Goddess turn their attention to her, fixating on something Sara did not know she could, something that she did not think to consider. Right now, their eyes press into her, and the pulsing from the floor returns, stronger than before. Sara panics at the mighty vibrations beneath her feet and thinks the cause is the Goddess.

However, no one else appears to be alarmed by this, nor do they seem to have noticed how the ground trembles. They do nothing other than watch Sara struggle to keep her footing. She soon steps forward, thinking the source may have been some machinery below their feet. Yet, she soon sees that this is not the case as the tremoring ground continues to follow her. While Sara endures this unsettling sensation, the overhead lights suddenly begin to flicker and buzz, soon bringing Mr. Davenport's focus to rest upon her.

"Just try to relax," he says while slowly approaching.

This simple phrase and movement instantly sparked more concern within Sara than anything in the past days could ever induce. It leaves her to notice how Charles and the Goddess watch her struggle with the commotion surrounding her and the internal issues becoming more present. Fear flutters uncontrollably within Sara's chest as the ground roars and the lights cut out. For a short moment, Sara still believes she is the only one experiencing this miraculous feat. However, everyone becomes susceptible to unpredictable motion. Parts and other unidentifiable things fly about and ultimately crash into the ground, soon encasing Sara in an isolated area. It leaves her to stand motionless in what she knows to be the components of Mr. Davenport's satellite. She freezes from nothing more than her fear in the epicenter of the mammoth storm.

CHAPTER FOURTEEN

The air turned crisp, and the sea breeze became intense, whipping various objects through the air like blades, turning them into deadly projectiles. Although, it does not compare to how the water crashes into the sides of the cargo ship. With each powerful collision, the sound sent through the colossal space would be enough to make one believe that the vessel would violently tear open. As the ship continues on its path and through the rough waters, the sight of the green sky and the massively wide eye of the storm reaches over the entirety of the feeder ship. Sparks of bright blue and white electricity fill the air as if warning anyone within the grasp of the hurricane-like event. However, anyone near this devastating cloud does not appear to have the best odds, especially as the full extent of the time warp presented as a storm causes the water to swallow everything in its wake.

The intimidating sea churns and seems to have a bright blue luminescent glow as it ravages the ship and makes multiple attempts to claim the craft for itself. Yet, how the feeder moves across the large waves affects the water's ability to take the lives onboard. It refuses to give the sea the right to capture the light of those within the ship. However, it does not seem like it is just how the water gets used to the crew's advantage. There is something about this ship that betters the raging ocean. Perhaps it is how the vessel itself appears to be shuddering beyond control. Something has intervened and safeguards the craft, the irreplaceable cargo, and those that roam within it. It allows the boat to maintain its current path and ability to avoid its untimely destruction.

THE LIGHTS INCONSISTENTLY cut in and out, giving Sara a glimpse into what horrors will happen before her. However, it does not appear to be much use as the ship constantly shifts due to the raging waters, hurling everyone on board about. It slams their bodies into one another as well as the surrounding objects. Luckily, no one seems to be injured. Yet, it is likely that someone will get hurt in the crazed thrashing in the coming moments.

"Sara!" Charles calls from what seems to be the distance.

Sara's focus turns to where she believes Charles to be and tries to head in that direction. However, her legs fail and trip on the unseen objects below her feet. She tries to push past whatever restricts her, although Sara cannot free herself. Before she panics, Sara returns her attention to where she heard Charles's voice originate.

"Charles," she eventually replies, hoping somehow to reassure him.

She continues to wiggle, trying to free herself from what had its grasp on her, and eventually breaks away from whatever this piece of rubble is. Sara instantly attempts to come to stand and make her way over the fallen debris. However, the ship takes another external hit. The cabin rocks violently, sending almost everybody sliding across the floor and slamming into the steel-lined walls. The screams of anguish made Sara's chest pound, and the floor roared again like it would split open. It seems to Sara that the surrounding area is responding to the horror alongside her. Yet, Sara forces herself to let this intense thought go, instantly thinking she is insane.

She climbs over the many bits of rubble caught under her feet and starts for Charles before the lights suddenly flick on. Just as Sara believes that the power will cut out again, she is thankfully proven wrong, giving her insight into where she should be heading. However, she does wish that she would not have to bear the ugly sight awaiting her. Men and women fighting off their screams and dealing with the pain and terror of their nightmare-like reality.

"Sara!" Charles shouts again.

She forcefully turns her line of sight toward Charles only to note how he holds a piece of machinery off his chest, with his arms caught between himself and the hunk of metal. It instantly causes Sara to find her feet and sprint in his direction. However, the ship takes another dip, leaving her to fight the gravity of the extreme angle. Yet, another pulse shoots across the floor, almost stabilizing the world around them. Before Sara can focus on how strange this occurrence is, she takes off for Charles.

As she reaches him, her hands lift toward the hunk of metal and wires, trying to free him from its hold. However, once she tugs on the device, she realizes she will not do such a thing. It is too large and heavy for her alone to maneuver. She momentarily pulls her hands away from the device and inspects it, wondering if there is anything she can do to free him. Yet, she does not know if there is anything she can do. In this instance, her face must have said the same thing as Charles's sinks in the very same manner.

"It's okay...." he tries.

"No! Don't!" Sara says, knowing what he is trying to do.

Sara looks around. However, her panic does not allow her to see anything. Sara ultimately returns her attention. She must be here for Charles.

"There's always something we can do," she dismisses, still thinking.

She turns, thinking that something in their immediate vicinity can aid in this situation. However, there does not appear to be anything of use. Yet, there are plenty of people. Perhaps they can help. Sara looks out to all the faces that might be able to spare a moment of their time in this crisis.

However, they all appear preoccupied with dealing with the issues surrounding them. Sara's eyes skim across the rocky floor to see Mr. Davenport trying to help his men just out of Sara's view. Although, it is as though he can sense her gaze, as though he can feel it gnawing at him. Mr. Davenport turns only to see that Sara stares his way. Spotting the urgency on Sara's expression leaves him to quickly return his attention to what he was doing before bouncing up and heading for Sara. He pauses, noting the thing pressed against Charles, although he pushes past this and speeds up.

"What can I do?" Mr. Davenport asks as he reaches them.

"Just pull," Sara demands as she yanks at the device.

Before he can even question their animalistic method, Mr. Davenport begins to aid Sara in her efforts, pulling with all his might. They both physically strain themselves, trying to drag the device away before Charles can finally move his arms enough to help them. As he begins to push, their eyes almost simultaneously close as they press and pull against the cold and dense metal. Before they have a chance to realize it, others have noticed and joined. They pull from one side and push from the other, all attempting to free Charles from his helplessly pinned state.

"Push!" one of the others says, triggering their attention.

Although their focus had briefly pulled away from their task, their strength had not eased. They press on, allowing the machinery to inch further and further away. Charles soon breathes a sigh of relief as he escapes the clutches of the dense hunk of steel. Although, he does not make it very far. Charles has collapsed to the ground, sending another wave of vibrations rocketing through the floor.

"Charles!" Sara panics.

She throws herself to the floor to him, wanting to know what is wrong with him. Once she comes face to face with him, Sara notices the exhausted expression that wears him down. It does not take long for Mr. Davenport to lower himself down to their side, wanting to help in any way he can. Although, she ignores him.

"Charles!" she says again with more urgency.

He tries to answer, although he is unable to. His lips constantly form and reform, attempting to get words out. However, it is of no use. Charles fights the urge to be sick, forcing his mouth to close and sluggishly turning away from Sara. As Sara realizes that there is not much she can do and cannot think of anything to aid him, she ultimately turns her attention to Mr. Davenport.

"What do we do?" she asks, thinking he might know what Charles is undergoing.

However, she can only watch as Mr. Davenport's face fills with nothing except uncertainty. He soon begins to lightly shake his head as if trying to warn Sara not to get her hopes up. Sara exhaled and noticed the pain in her chest. Yet, she does not pay much attention to this agonizing sensation as her focus mainly lies with Charles. While she still awaits Mr. Davenport's pending answer, Sara cannot help but note how Charles continues to struggle with whatever has its hold on him.

"I don't know right now," Mr. Davenport eventually says softly, as though he knows of the disappointment this statement will undoubtedly bring her.

Sara is understandably disappointed by this. Charles needs help, more help than she can offer him. Yet, Sara still wants to do everything she can for him. He does not deserve this. Not after everything he has done for everyone else.

"We can't leave him like this," Sara says as she looks about, noticing how the supposed Great One is not present at such an event.

Before becoming lost in this anger-evoking observation, Sara returns her focus to what she was trying to accomplish. She scans the area around them, hoping to find anything that could at least shield Charles from the damage caused by the ongoing storm. However, Sara cannot find anything better than the machine that had trapped him in the first place. With this thought fresh on her mind, Sara resumes her search, although she has modified it slightly.

She looks for something that could potentially barricade the hefty device, preventing the potentially fatal incident Charles had endured. Sara's eyes almost instantly fixated on the scattered scaffolding she had watched the workers use not long ago. Perhaps they could be used as a barrier, protecting Charles from getting crushed again while they use the large machine to shield him from anything else that could endanger him until they escape the eye of the hurricane.

"Here, help me," Sara says.

"Help you what?" Mr. Davenport cannot help but ask.

Mr. Davenport looks over to Sara as she speedily heads for the unevenly stacked pieces of metal before he can moderately understand what she is after. Yet, he soon gets to his feet and aids Sara, picking up the loose poles and railings as he can. However, Davenport stops, noticing how Sara has frozen in place, fixated on something that Mr. Davenport has not caught on to yet. He pauses, wondering what could have caused her to cease her efforts to help Charles.

However, his face droops, understanding what caused her reaction. He listens to the fading sounds of the storm and breathes as he relaxes to the sudden ease beneath their feet. The hurricane is finally passing, freeing them from their likely untimely deaths.

"It's over," Sara whispers.

While she knows that the destruction has ceased, Sara takes a moment to inspect the mess and agony surrounding her. It is something she now realizes to be pointless. Sara notes the blood the workers wear alongside their broken expressions. Pained, Sara turns her attention to the floor, where she finds the debris from the satellite that Mr. Davenport and the people surrounding her had worked on for longer than she could fathom. She notes how they are unevenly scattered about and focuses on where she knew she was when the storm had come over them, where she had collapsed.

This thought brings her pain as it prevents her from helping those surrounding her. With her anger and other unflattering emotions rising, Sara lifts her line of sight. However, this seems to be a mistake as Sara realizes that the only thing missing from this freshly settled space is the woman Sara would have expected to have gloating, looking down her nose at Mr. Davenport: The Goddess.

"I think we must have made it," Mr. Davenport says from behind.

Sara's eyes are the first to find Mr. Davenport, slowly gazing toward him with what seems like cold daggers before her body almost snakes around on the spot. She is not enthused by how things unfolded. It nearly cost lives. It could still cost Charles's life. The gradual and distant way Sara had turned to him reminded Mr. Davenport of another woman of great potential. He is reminded of the Great Goddess with her cold and angered demeanor that may affect anyone within her immediate range. However, Mr. Davenport soon lets this terrifying moment go as Sara's expression changes, leaving her with her more familiar and comforting essence that he has become accustomed to. Although, he cannot help but notice that there still appears to be a touch of something left behind. Something bitter, angered, and reserved.

"I guess so," Sara says as she heads back to Charles's side. "Remind me again, why thought that would be a good idea."

Mr. Davenport's face flushes with regret as his mouth opens, muted, knowing that he can only watch as Sara stalks past him. Although Sara knows it must have sparked pain on Mr. Davenport's behalf, she does not care. Her focus needs to rest on Charles, the man caught in a war that he should not need to burden. It is a pointless war between Mr. Davenport and the Great One. As Sara draws closer to Charles, she notes that his body has kindly been moved thanks to the people who helped free him. He now sits, resting against the contraption that had him trapped, beginning to crush him. Once Sara slowly kneels beside him, Charles's eyes flicker, attempting to remain awake, more for her sake than his own. Although, it appears as though he is failing in his efforts.

"Hey," Sara says, hoping to capture his attention. "How are you feeling?"

Charles's eyes widen enough to tell her he has registered his presence, though they soon glue shut despite his will against the fact. The sight pains Sara deeply, though she soon lifts her focus to those surrounding them. She fixates on the closest man to her, looking him in the eye, hoping he may know how to help Charles.

"What can we do?" she asks.

No one answers her immediately. However, the looks between the men and women offer Sara a sliver of hope. Once the unspoken banter between these workers eventually eases, they allow their attention to fall back onto Sara and the newly unconscious Charles.

"I think the only thing we can do is take him to the med bay.... And hope that our doctor wasn't injured in the storm," one of the men replies.

"Alright," Sara agrees.

As Sara appears as though she were going to help move him, the workers return their gaze to her with something sympathetic resting on them. The same man puts his arm out and lightly rests it on Sara's forearm, gently letting her know he is there. She looks at him with worry, although Sara's expression softens once she notices how this man softly gazes at her.

"It's okay, we'll take him," the man assures.

She pauses for a moment, considering what this man has offered. However, she appears to be shaking off this suggestion, not wanting to leave Charles's side. With the Goddess gone, being on board Mr. Davenport's cargo ship, Charles will need her there with him.

"I don't want to leave him alone," Sara dismisses.

"It's alright.... After what happened, I don't think we will be in any hurry to leave him," he continues.

Sara pauses again, realizing that this man truly means well. Perhaps it would be better for Charles if Sara would continue on the journey, working alongside Mr. Davenport and the Goddess, to make the best decision. As Sara slowly understands this, she releases a long breath and allows her eyes to return their gaze to this man.

"Make sure he's alright, will you?" Sara hopes.

"We will," he agrees.

Sara reluctantly lets Charles leave her side, watching these men haul him away. However, she knows that this is for the best. Sara must know what Mr. Davenport was thinking when he decided to put his ship and his men aboard through such a deadly hurricane. Not to mention finding where the Goddess has run off to when they all needed her and when she could have proved she is the one worth trusting.

Yet, Sara knows she must focus on what is before her. She turns to Mr. Davenport, knowing that he floats behind her. Just waiting.

"What was that?" Sara asks.

Mr. Davenport slowly lifts his eyes to her, wanting to tell Sara everything and hide the horrible truth from her. He opens his mouth to answer. However, Sara's thoughts fade away. She pivots on the spot and lifts her head to the space above them, back to where the deck and command console lie, to where they were when all this started.

"What is it?" Mr. Davenport questions, sensing the urgency that seemingly expels from her.

"Well, I guess I'm about to find out," she says as she heads toward the exit, toward the numerous staircases.

While her mind races, thinking through many possibilities and wondering when the full scope of what transpires will finally draw to a close, Sara's head swirls. She is still unsure how to navigate the sudden enhancement of her abilities. It leaves her to struggle with the lightheadedness that comes with it. Although she pushes past this advanced version of motion sickness, knowing that the floor above is where they will find the Goddess. And hopefully, the answers that they all need that she is sure to bring.

CHAPTER FIFTEEN

Standing out on the open deck would leave Sara in this constant fear and child-like vulnerability. However, at this moment, whatever had alerted her to the Goddess's whereabouts and the temper she stews disallows Sara to her usual cocktail of emotions. It strangely gives Sara a similar essence to what the Goddess carries through her every day. Yet, Sara does not allow this overwhelming power to affect her. Not in the way that she suspects that it does for the Goddess. More considering the intoxicating manner. It almost speaks to her as if it is trying to persuade Sara.

She pushes past the surge of thoughts and emotions that have begun to overpower her once she notices the Great One inside the control room. The woman looks out the window, facing Sara's way. Their eyes meet. However, Sara cannot help but notice the warning in the Goddess's eye.

Yet, she is unable to place what this warning could be. It is not at all threatening like Sara would have once thought. However, with Sara's heightened ability, she has reason to believe it to be a concern. It almost beckons Sara and draws her in despite her knowing the dangers.

"Do you want me to come with you?" Mr. Davenport asks from behind, taking Sara by surprise.

Despite this surprise, Sara steps forward, wanting to get the following over and done with. However, she does not give Mr. Davenport a chance to tag along. After what everyone on board had just experienced, Sara could not forgive him quite yet.

"I'll let you know," Sara eventually says, already coming to reach the entrance to the control room. "Wait there for me, will you?"

Sara notes the disappointment in Mr. Davenport's eyes as she closes the door behind her, although she knows it is pointless to tell him anything else. He cannot ease the situation between herself and the Goddess. He will be good at keeping watch, hopefully preventing anything else from escalating.

"You seemed to have faired well," the Goddess states before Sara even has time to face her.

However, this does pull Sara's focus away from the inaudible and almost desperate plea of Mr. Davenport. It leaves Sara to take in the bright space before her. Momentarily ignoring the woman, she takes her time to note the surrounding area. Noticing that the only damage this room appears to have seen is the wall lined with office chairs. Though, few seem to be damaged. Sara notices that most of them are in tacked.

Yet, she cannot help but let her mind fill with the simple thought of rest and that she has not had time to rest since first meeting Charles. Since first being brought into this crazed world. Sara misses her bed and the warmth of her father's bar. It always felt like home to her.

Once realizing that the attention has been placed on their surroundings more than it should be, Sara finally looks the Goddess in the eyes. The seemingly distressed appearance burns behind the Great One expression and puts Sara on edge. Although, everything about this woman seems to put Sara on edge.

"So have you," she soon replies.

Something flashes across the Goddess's expression, momentarily wiping the agony clear. However, whatever this flicker is, it disappears too fast to be caught. It leaves Sara to miss this glimpse of whatever the Goddess has lying beneath her stone-like and usually collected surface.

Although, this does not seem to bother Sara in the slightest. She slowly walks over to the wall and picks up the nearest chair. She corrects its positioning before taking a seat and slowly rolling toward the Goddess.

While Sara takes her time to make herself comfortable, the Goddess watches on, knowing she cannot bring herself to hurry things along, not with Sara anyway. Yet, the wait gives the Goddess a chance to properly deal with the various thoughts that could lead to an issue between herself and Sara despite the fact there already appear to be multiple in place. However, the Goddess can shrug off this restraining realization and think of a better way to approach her current situation with Sara.

"Yes. I tried to correct things from here," the Goddess begins. "Yet, it does appear that what happened was beyond my control."

Sara stares blankly at the woman before her, unsure how to proceed. Deciding whether or not it would be wise to confront the Great One on several matters, abandoning herself and Charles for one. However, she believes it may be better for all if Sara plays along nicely with the Goddess.

"How noble," Sara says while spinning around on the office chair like a small child, trying to make light of the situation.

Once Sara retains her original positioning in the seat, she allows her expression of humor to fade and her arms to fold. Staring into the Goddess's seemingly empty eyes leaves Sara in this new state of curiosity, wanting more than anything to know what the Goddess truly wants. She must know what the Great Goddess had planned for Sara.

"What do we do now?" Sara asks genuinely.

The slow and seemingly calculated head tilt this woman does sends chills down Sara's spine. As if this warns her of whatever may unfold next. Yet, it does not discourage her. It cements that Sara must intervene in whatever the Goddess's master plan may be.

"We reach shore, then we will head for my home...." The Great One begins. "Once there, we will begin the transfer of power over to you."

Although the Goddess believes that she has given the answer that Sara seeks, she is ultimately proven wrong as Sara's face sinks in nothing more than disappointment. While Sara's head nods, the Goddess stews on the endless possibilities that may run through Sara's mind. Their bond grows stronger but tears them apart. As Sara's abilities grow in the Goddess's absence, the Goddess's seem to wither away.

"I will need to show you.... It is one to tell you. Though it will be meaningless unless you understand what we are speaking of," the Great Goddess attempts to explain.

While it was clear that this woman tried to give context, Sara's confusion could not be more raised than it is at this time. Her brows are together as she tries to understand the small communication she has received from the Goddess. A part of Sara wants the Goddess to be honest with her. However, another part of Sara knows how disastrous that can be. Besides, Sara does not want this world to be real anymore. It only brings death, and Sara knows she cannot stop it. Not unless she receives the talents the Goddess welds.

"So, we get to your temple.... Then I'll finally understand what it is we're doing. That still seems a little vague," Sara says as she straightens her posture.

Their eyes remain trained on one another for a long moment as if trying to read the other's mind or get insight into what they are dealing with. However, it breaks as the Goddess nods toward the encasing window, revealing the strip of land that they close in on.

"Is.... Is that....?" Sara tries.

A faint smile stretches across the Goddess's face, offering a glimpse of the woman's bliss. However, she wipes it from her expression before slightly turning toward Sara.

"It is my home, my sanctuary," the Goddess clarifies.

Sara is distracted by a lump in her throat. She immediately tries to rid it by conventional means. However, it appears as though it will not pass any time soon. Once she settles with the uncomfortable sensation within her throat, Sara notices how the sweat forms in her hands and slowly trickles down them. As she tries to wipe them, a bubbling occurs in her stomach. Yet, this is something Sara has dealt with before. It is something she knows. A warning of sorts. One that forces her attention to turn toward the Goddess in expectation.

"We should get Charles," the Goddess states. "He will want to be there when we land…. When we begin the transfer."

Regret and worry make a comeback, starting to weigh Sara down. However, she pushes past this, knowing that she must. It is a warning to confirm this to her.

While she knows that whatever happens next will not be ideal, Sara stands and looks the Great One in the eye. Although the Goddess is still capable of many feats, it does not take much to notice the agony that Sara has begun to endure. It strikes the Great One as odd. The Goddess is more than aware of this overbearing sensation that claims the user.

"Is there a problem?" the Goddess questions.

"Yeah…. As it so happens, there is. And I know you're not going to like it," Sara says as she heads for the door, knowing that the Goddess follows.

SARA AND THE GODDESS stand by Charles's head, worrying that there is something worse than what lies in front of them happening beneath the surface. Especially given his pale and shrunken appearance and the dark circles that threaten to swallow his eyes. Although, there is not much that they can do for him now. The only thing they can do in this situation is to carry out their plan, and both the Goddess and Sara know this. It only causes their unbearable tension to rise.

"What happened?" the woman asks.

Sara pauses as she crosses her arm over her chest, considering the best way to answer. However, she cannot help but allow her eyes to dig into the Goddess.

"Well, he was almost crushed to death, pinned between a wall and the satellite," Sara says, with anger beginning to burn through her words despite her best intentions. "But you tried to stop it.... Right? It's why you were up there and not down here with the rest of us."

Although Sara planned to remain neutral and follow the Goddess's lead, she abandoned that mentality as she could not permit the Goddess an escape from what she could have prevented. She and Charles were beside each other when the lights first went out. She left him to fend for himself with nothing that compares to her ability.

Sara's words frightened the Goddess into thinking of Charles. The Great One's eyes lift and hang in the air as she slowly notes the weight of her statement. Once the woman collects herself, her body gradually swoops in Sara's direction.

"Is there something you want to say to me, Sara?" the Goddess questions.

After a slight pause, Sara's lips purse, wondering if she could correct the path that she has taken. She relaxes her lips once she realizes that her approach is too intense for what is needed for everyone. Especially Charles. He needs her to be there for the Goddess, to better the world as Sara knows he truly wants. Despite knowing that whatever the Goddess plans is too dangerous for anyone to endure.

"What is there to say?" Sara eventually replies.

"Perhaps you are unhappy with my methods," the woman suggests, her eyes lingering, almost pressing into Sara's.

A smile stretches across Sara's face, leaving the Goddess to dwell on whatever Sara holds onto despite her realization. However, neither one of them appears to attempt to mend this immense yet unspoken damage. They remain silent, focused on Charles before the Goddess makes her way through the exit.

The expression of shock that soon becomes fixed on Sara's face brings the Goddess great joy from a glimpse over her shoulder. Yet, it is short-lived as Sara trails behind, and they both bear witness to the many men who escort the seemingly intact satellite through the long and freshly swept corridor. The workers push the large device on some trolley-like contraption alongside the few forklifts that take the weight and force.

"He is still going ahead with it," the Goddess mutters half to herself.

Sara's eyes fixate on the woman, taking in her dread and the anger that honestly seems a little over the top. Sara watches her deal with the many things she cannot understand yet. However, she knows she will only be for a short time longer. Both offer relief and fear for whatever lies ahead.

"Of course, he is.... He's dreamed of doing this, trying to save the planet since his father's death," Sara says, revealing that she is more than aware of what has transpired in the past and the goddess part in it.

The Goddess does not bring herself to look at Sara, nor does she permit herself to respond in any way. She only watches as Mr. Davenport and his goons escort the machinery through the hanger. The fact that the Goddess does not react to Sara's statement and the satellite that threatens to destroy all that the Goddess works for brings Sara an abundance of confusion. She struggles with this act of bafflement, trying to figure out what runs through the Goddess's mind. However, it does not aid in this situation. Sara still does not find an answer to why the woman would only stare at something that can only lead to falter in her plans.

"Aren't you going to do something?" Sara finally questions.

The Great One walks down the nearest staircase with her shoulders pinned back tight before eventually believing it is wise to include Sara in her reasoning.

"There is not much to do," the woman begins. "He will not be able to accomplish much without you poised in the seat of power.... He has informed you that he wishes you to be in the seat of power, yes?"

"So.... You both want me to become you? To be Mother Nature?" she asks, feeling the need to stress the weight of what was said.

The Goddess continues, striding toward Mr. Davenport as he watches his life's work roll past him. However, his line of sight is soon triggered as the Goddess slows to a stop, placing herself by his side. Fear sparks for Sara and Mr. Davenport, thinking this woman will do something everyone will regret. Yet, nothing appears to happen. No flying objects, no screaming, or power cuts. Nothing immediate, at least.

"I trust that you will not damage the Amazon in the way you have done previously," the Great Goddess states blankly.

While the Goddess's tone alerts him to her seemingly permeant displeased manner, Mr. Davenport takes a breath as he realizes that this conversation is to prevent an uncomfortable situation, not political as he suspected. Once he takes a breath, Mr. Davenport tucks his hands into his pant pockets and allows himself to look the Goddess in the eye.

"Everything will be left undamaged," he reassures. "We'll move it to our launch sight nearby."

"Which is where exactly, Mr. Davenport?" she questions. "If I am not mistaken, I believe there are very few places in the world where it is safe to launch such things. Although, I do not have vast knowledge of such things."

Mr. Davenport smiles at her concern before focusing on Sara. He hopes to get a glimpse of the familiar version of her that he was lucky enough to speak sense into. Lucky enough to be given a chance to reveal the horrible truths surrounding the Goddess and all that she entails. However, he is wrong regarding Sara's overall essence. She remains relatively closed off and reserved. Once Mr. Davenport deals with his brief disappointment, he comes to return his attention to the Goddess.

"I don't think that you'll have to worry about that; we have a.... safe method in place for such circumstances," he finishes.

The Goddess does not believe him. However, it does not bother Mr. Davenport. He does not need her to trust him. The only trust he seeks is from Sara. He needs her to. Unfortunately, he may have burned that bridge already.

"Hem.... Safe?" the Goddess parrots.

"Yes," Mr. Davenport confirms.

While Sara is still at odds with the Goddess and Mr. Davenport, she cannot help but smirk at their awkward encounter. Although, she soon wipes her expression clean, not wanting to give either of them the wrong impression.

Like Mr. Davenport, Sara turns her gaze to the workers guiding the satellite to what appears to be a scissor lift by the end of the hanger. Though, Sara does not stay long. She turns and practically runs up the stairs, not wanting to remain in her current state. Sara waits for everyone around her to make decisions regarding her future. Sara does not want to be in this constant limbo as she has endured since first meeting Charles.

"Miss Bornstein!" Mr. Davenport calls from below.

Knowing that if she were to stop to answer him, she would not continue, Sara does not look back. She keeps for the door, noting the heaviness of the stare that she knows is pressed into the back of her skull by the Goddess. It almost digs into her skin, making her more than a little uncomfortable. However, she is free from this sensation once her feet cross the invisible line separating the ship's intestines and the outer deck.

Sara continues to walk across the open space, mindful of the debris that litter the ground. Yet, her eyes eventually come to a close, causing Sara to stop in her tracks to take a moment to collect herself. However, her moment of bliss is interrupted by a faint purr and the sound of what seems to be the howling wind and bubbling of water. Although it is not soft, they almost roar, leaving Sara to reopen her eyes and search for the cause. After almost immediately ruling out the possibility of anything onboard the ship, Sara takes several steps forward, coming to reach the end of the cargo ship. Despite the tense knot in her chest, Sara leans forward to note what is the source of the serial commotion.

CHAPTER SIXTEEN

Sara stands in nothing other than awe, staring directly at the water below. She watches as it seems to evaporate into thin air. However, Sara knows that it does not. It merely separates down the middle of the canal, making way for the concrete and metallic platform that rises from beneath it. The stage ascends vertically, shooting above the waterline before the divided sections collapse and conjoin at the center. While this podium-like piece of machinery continues to reach its intended state, Sara notes how the platform almost meets the side of the feeder ship. It leaves Sara to wonder about the full extent of the crazed operation. Yet, this thought is lost once she steps back with worry suddenly fluttering within her chest. She believes this occurrence may impact the ship, threatening those who have been through more than enough. However, Sara soon settles as the platform finally slows before it appears to come to a stop, sitting parallel to the deck.

"What's next?" Sara sarcastically asks herself.

After taking a breath, trying to compensate for the terror she had just endured, Sara turns back towards the door. She freezes, and her breaths cease again due to the unnerving sight of Mr. Davenport and the Goddess awaiting her.

"Well.... I take it that this is your doing," Sara says to Mr. Davenport as she lightly gestures toward the platform.

Mr. Davenport cannot help himself. He lets out a deep chuckle at Sara's fairly normalized state. Although, he is quick to silence himself in the Goddess's overly intimidating presence. Especially after noticing how she continues to dig her eyes into his skull. The Great One is trying to discourage anything that may corrupt Sara's perception or interference that could spoil what the Goddess plans to do with Sara once she reaches the land.

"You could say that," he eventually replies.

Sara momentarily pulls her attention away, focusing on the large dais intended for something important, something integral to what Mr. Davenport has in place. Her line of sight remains here for another beat, triggering impatience within the Goddess and worry within Mr. Davenport. However, they are both soon put to ease as she slowly returns her gaze to their tense faces.

"What is it?" Sara asks, feeling the need to ask.

The expression on Mr. Davenport's face gradually darkens, thinking of a way to explain what he plans on doing without the Goddess conflicting with it. Yet, he soon realizes there is no way to tell Sara the truth without including the Great One. However, Mr. Davenport still thinks that it would be better for the moment to find a way to explain things without telling them the whole truth. Compartmentalization and redirection. No matter how much it pains him to stoop to the Goddess's restrictive level. He will be the one who tells her the truth and protects her from the unnecessary danger that she will endure.

"That, Miss Bronstein, is something put in place for such an occasion," he begins. "Complete courtesy to the cooperation between the American and Brazilian governments."

While Sara appears to be mildly impressed by the lengths everyone went to for such an incident, the expression upon the Goddess does not seem as enthused. Not that this comes as a surprise for everyone involved in the uncomfortable ever-going situation.

"You have spoiled sacred grounds, Mr. Davenport," the Goddess says with her words shaped and carefully chosen.

Mr. Davenport takes time to gather his comeback for the Goddess. Although, to his disappointment, there does not seem to be much in the way of responses. No quips that could break the tension that continues to rise and inform the Great One to the truth. The only option he could muster in this short time is pure honesty. However, that does not mean the Goddess will listen.

"Fortunately, I have not done anything of the sort this time.... Dame Nature," he says. "This was put in place long before I was a part of anything that could disrupt any of your.... Earthly contributions."

The Goddess's eyes flash with fury, and shoulders pull back a little tighter than they have been. Although, Mr. Davenport does not seem concerned with the display of irritation on her behalf. Yet, this does not appear to extend to Sara. Her chest and cheeks flush in expectance, thinking that the Goddess will end up doing something that no one will be able to come back from. However, the Great One soon allows herself to be calm enough to speak without the risk of lashing out. Giving Sara a brief look at the woman she had first encountered, the woman that Sara is sure lies somewhere beneath the intervention of the mind-altering abilities.

"And why is that? Why would the American and Brazilian governments do such a thing without probable cause? What would be the use?" the goddess questions.

The silence on Mr. Davenport's part leaves Sara with an overly uncomfortable sensation bubbling in her stomach, warning her of what he must be planning to divulge and the issues it may cause. She watches his face and how his smile fills with emotional agony and warming pride. However, it does not quite compare to how Mr. Davenport's turmoil soon stretches from him to her. Air disappears from her lungs, and Sara's head flicks back. While she attempts to get her breathing back in order, sweat trickles down to her fingertips despite the cold rush that overwhelms her. It encases her, surrounding her until Sara is on the verge of becoming unconscious.

"Yes, well.... It was put in place after my father sent a request for you to be monitored by higher authorities. I think we both know what happened to him in the end. However, I don't believe you know about the military's interventions after what you did to dispose of him. Of your problem," Mr. Davenport explains with more prominence in his final statement, digging into the Goddess. "Why do you think that I was in such a good position with them since then? And why I am the one they would turn to when it came down to you and your operations?"

The Goddess's silence almost forces Sara to step back toward the end of the deck. She focuses firmly on where she could only suspect the Goddess's home and temple to be. Her eyes lightly graze over the area with something calling to her. However, it does not appear like anything that particularly stands out to Sara. Not that Sara would have expected it to in the first place. Yet, she would have expected some movement within the trees, a light breeze. Sara's eyes widen as she realizes what she is supposed to bear witness to. The ravishing of the foliage, moving in a violent and threatening manner, leaves Sara to fear for those who await the Goddess.

Unfortunately, Sara thinks they may be in danger and believes that the Goddess will be their untimely end. Sara instantly combs her mind, trying to find a solution. However, there do not seem to be many options. Feeling almost defeated by the lack of freedom, Sara returns to the Goddess's side with faint hopes to calm the woman.

Once noticing that the conversation between the Goddess and Mr. Davenport may continue on its dangerous path, Sara steps forward. Sara claims the attention of the Great One and allows relief to flash across Mr. Davenport's expression. However, it does not go as planned. She stands frozen, trying to conjure something to pull the Goddess's primary focus away from the tension between herself and Mr. Davenport.

"When were you planning on leaving?" Sara asks the moment her mind finally clicks. Although, it spilled out in a faster manner than she would have hoped for.

The Goddess's expression slowly softens, sensing something off with Sara. The Great One focuses on Sara's eyes and assumes her awkwardness is because of their location. However, she also realizes that the internal conflict within Sara may be from the struggles that come with the divine power that has begun to claim Sara for its own.

"When we can depart...." The Goddess says in a controlled way.

Sara knows it took a lot from the Goddess to say this in that way. There is something else the Goddess wants to discuss. However, they are aware that this is not going to happen, not now. There is too much at stake.

"Right," Sara puffs.

After this immensely awkward and overly tense encounter between them, they all simultaneously turn their attention to the sudden opening of a large hatch further down the ship. It gives a straight shot from the hanger below to the deck their feet stand firmly on. However, Sara does not allow herself to pay much attention to what takes place before her. She lets her mind drift for a moment, forgetting all the trouble that they have been experiencing throughout the past few days and the weather phenomena that have lasted weeks. Although, the more she allows herself to dwell on nothingness, the more she realizes the full extent of what plays out. More so for Mr. Davenport and the Goddess. It has been years.

Sara pushes these thoughts free from her mind. She needs time to clear the mess that has taken over her life. With this, she watches the various men move about the deck, preparing for the move. However, her attention is soon triggered by the small crane-like machine being moved and placed into an ideal spot for maneuvering such a hefty device. While Sara notes how her breaths within her chest seem heavy, the machine slowly lowers before reemerging with the satellite.

With a dull throbbing in the base of her skull, Sara turns, surveying the area filled with many workers and numerous bits of equipment. Yet, her focus rests on the crane ready to lift the machinery onto the platform. A soft breath of air is released from her nose, probably intended to be a laugh. However, it does not take.

Mr. Davenport catches onto Sara's current displeasure, noticing how she has begun to carry herself. While she was showing a few signs of the Goddess's familiar persona, he could not help but see himself in her at this very moment. The dark circles that surround her eyes, the fake smile, and forcefully pinned back shoulders, trying to convince those around her they are stronger and more haled together than they are.

Mr. Davenport wishes he could tell Sara what she needs to know before stepping into the rainforest. Warn her of the dangers that come with stepping out there with the Goddess, receiving those abilities, and what may happen to her if the Goddess gets what she needs from Sara. Although, Mr. Davenport knows that it is all moot now anyway. Whatever he thinks he knows or the connections that have led them all here. It will all come down to Sara. His personal preferences and interactions with Sara will have no value once they are on the Goddess's land. It is a matter of belief in right and wrong.

"You don't need to worry, Miss Borstein. Once the satellite is aboard the launch pad, we can hop on one of our disembarking vessels. Make a start for that rainforest over there," Mr. Davenport offers, knowing full well of the anxiety she must be experiencing.

Sara's eyesight comes back to Davenport, hearing that this platform is for launch. Although, she does not seem surprised in the slightest. She expected as such with the scale of his operation. Yet, that does not change how she looks at Mr. Davenport. Plain, but still kind as she realizes that he wishes for the best outcome just as she does.

She soon nods lightly, ultimately agreeing to his generous offer. However, the Goddess does not appear to register what Sara and Mr. Davenport have agreed on. She still watches the men move the delicate machinery, firmly fixated on the satellite.

Yet, what frightens Sara and Mr. Davenport is that there appears to be something conflicted etched on her mind and her expression. However, the anger and hope that the Great One emanates capture Sara's full attention. She realizes that the conflict is something that Sara already knows of. The Goddess fights the almost uncontrollable urge that comes with the mind-altering, atmosphere-bending abilities. Perhaps the Goddess is not too far gone, too unpredictable and unreasonable, unlike what Sara was programmed to believe.

"Is everything okay?" Sara asks the Goddess.

The Great One slowly allows her line of sight to pull away from the satellite and the worker to fixate on Sara. However, the Goddess's mind is still elsewhere. It clouds her thoughts and whatever Sara will have to say.

"Of course," she replies despite the cloud hovering above them.

Sara and Mr. Davenport lift their attention to this miraculous and sudden dark storm cloud, obviously coming to the same conclusion. The Goddess has summoned it with the last remnant of her power. Yet, Mr. Davenport appears to be in denial in this serial situation, and the hairs on the back of Sara's neck prick up in expectance and terror on everyone's behalf.

"What are you doing?" Sara asks with stress over running her tone.

The Great One does not answer. Her attention is between both realities presented within her mind. Knowing of the dangerous compulsions that whisper to the Goddess, and that she is currently undergoing, Sara's focus flickers from the impending danger and the Goddess herself. She is trying to think of a way to intervene in this situation. However, Sara is not as quick to a solution as she wishes. The inconsistent flash of light within this cloud fills Sara with fear and the Goddess with what appears to be physical agony. Sara worries for the Goddess. The torment in the Goddess's head and the pain she is burdened with leave Sara to wonder what will aid this woman with divine intervention in play.

"We'll finish this. We'll head for your camp, put me in the seat of power as you would say, then I'll help you," Sara says, trying to appeal to the Goddess. "This isn't the way.... You could hurt those men."

With this, the Goddess's face turns red as it begins to stream with tears, and her teeth clench in agony as if hearing what Sara warns her of. However, Sara does not seem to acknowledge this. She focuses on the intensified pain that the Goddess emanates, both emotional and physical. The terror weighs Sara down, knowing that this is what the Goddess is currently undergoing, fighting an invisible enemy within herself and losing the battle. Yet, Sara pushes past this uncomfortable sensation, focusing on the Goddess's well-being and the lurking danger ahead.

"Goddess, please don't do it.... Please," Sara pleads.

The Goddess appears to relax, soon allowing her tears to lighten. It briefly offers Sara and Mr. Davenport a glimpse of the familiar and held-together woman they have come to know. Sara breathes at this relieving sight, and her shoulders slump at the seemingly calm essence expressed within the Goddess. However, Sara soon realizes why this must be and why something as powerful as the earthy spirit within the woman would suddenly appear calm in this time of uncertainty. It suggests that the power within the Goddess has gotten what it wants. It has its claim over the woman inside, taming her into doing its bidding.

"Wait," Sara begins with a flinch.

Although, it appears to be too late. A bright light suddenly cuts through the deck, colliding with the satellite at its center. Everyone on the deck gets thrown back due to the sheer force propelled upon them before the machinery erupts in flames.

Sara catapults herself forward, thinking of the men at the heart of the lightning strike. As Sara edges closer, wanting to move the workers away from the fire, another strike unexpectedly comes down upon the wreckage, followed by another. Before she knows it, Sara is back beside the Goddess and Mr. Davenport, and her mind fogs, and her vision blurs. The ache at the base of her skull alerts Sara to the reasoning behind it. Although, it does not help her with the trouble she faces. Her newly uneven state and the fact that the men she had just attempted to save are left to fend for themselves as lighting continues to rain down upon the wreckage and everything else in its vicinity.

"Stop," Sara demands despite the surge of nausea that overwhelms her.

However, it does not appear like these lightning strikes will subside anytime soon. Not that the Goddess will hear what Sara has to say in her current state, not in the way that Sara needs her to, not in the way that everyone needs her to. Just as Sara believes there will be no end, everything goes quiet. Sara and Mr. Davenport pause in silence, looking up to see the sky slowly clearing away. Everyone who is able turns to the burnt ash and the rubble left by the unnatural occurrence. Despite the rush of blood in the head and sickness, Sara is the first to return to her feet. While she knows that there is nothing that she can do for the men who unfortunately lost their lives in the Goddess's act of means, it does not stop Sara from gradually heading for the pile of nothingness.

Once Sara reaches the wreck, Mr. Davenport slowly approaches from behind, looking down at the scrap he had dedicated his life to. Sara turns to note the defeat and unbearable failure that has come to rest on his shoulders. Her heart goes out to him, not just for the sorrow that losing his men would undoubtedly bring, but knowing what this machine meant to him. Knowing that saving what his father gave his life for was everything Mr. Davenport had left. The internal agony in his eyes tells Sara that he no longer has anything left to hold onto, thanks to the power that surges through the Goddess's veins.

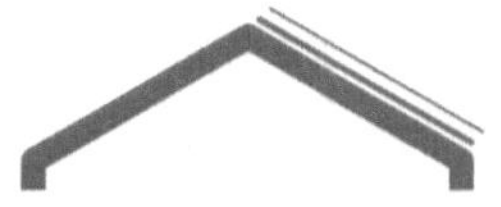

CHAPTER SEVENTEEN

It had taken a lot of convincing to get the newly deflated and seemingly lifeless Mr. Davenport to agree to allow Sara and the Goddess aboard one of his disembarking vessels. Not that it matters to him anymore. Mr. Davenport cannot do anything to change their situation, to influence anything the Goddess will do. He has lost his purpose and the connection he had to his father.

While Sara knows their journey toward the rainforest is for the best, she still cannot help but stew on the guilt and remorse that she has. She attempts to distract herself by staring at the fading image of the concrete and steel platform centered in the water. Sara watches it drift off into the distance. Yet, she cannot help but jolt back into her dreaded reality as the coarse motion of the small boat. It's inconsistently bouncing and tilting, nearly throwing Sara out of her seat.

"Ow," she softly puffs to herself.

As Sara must remain present within the daunting moments ahead and deal with the traumatizing events she has just endured, she thinks of the endless possibilities in the foliage ahead. She thinks of what she must take place in, her part in it, and the extent of what the Goddess wishes to do with Sara. It leaves her eyes to drift off in the Goddess's direction as if Sara would conclude this with a gaze at the Goddess's expression. However, this is not Sara's main concern once she notices the Goddess's appearance. There is no sign of the events that had just taken place, no shared remorse. The Goddess sits with her usual stone-like look. Sparking anger, frustration, and disappointment within Sara as she desperately wishes that she could get a glimpse of the woman trapped behind the unperceivable power she possesses.

"How long will this take?" Sara asks as she takes her attention away. She does not want to give the Goddess everything she wants. Not yet. "The trip, the transfer.... Whatever I must do afterward."

However, the Goddess would not have noticed Sara's displeasure and lack of wanting to be within the same vicinity as the Goddess. More because the woman's line of sight remains firmly trained on the rainforest, clearly finding herself caught in mid-thought. Or searching for something within the rainforest, her temple; it calls to her, bringing her into itself like a beacon.

"Not too long," the Great One ultimately says in short.

Sara nods even though she is aware that she is the only one who knows of the movement, that the Goddess cannot see the faint signs of disdain and the distance in Sara's eyes. Perhaps she had only made a nod to somewhat reassuring herself in this time of uncertainty. Yet, Sara is brought out of her lapse in focus as she notes the Goddess's obsession with whatever lies behind the trees and thinks back to when it had called upon her. It had spoken to her, trying to warn of what lies ahead. Sara wants nothing more than to hear the said warning. However, she knows she must not, not in such a dire situation. Sara cannot help but soon think of the lives lost in their journey and the many more that could die due to this continuously unfolding drama. She cannot permit herself to let that be in vain.

"This has all happened so fast.... but it feels like I've been waiting forever," Sara mutters.

THE WET SQUELCHING beneath Sara's feet leaves her with an overly gross and jittery sensation in her stomach. More because it is a far cry from the familiar streets of New York. However, Sara soon pushes past this uncomfortable feeling as there is something particularly familiar to her about this place like she has returned home after a long time away. Sara does not even need to pause and wait for the Goddess to lead her the way. She walks without guidance, straight into the heart of the miniature civilization. Straight into what Sara knows to be the Goddess's temple, her sanctuary, and where, thanks to her empathic abilities, Sara knows things will eventually play out.

Unable to permit herself to be anywhere near the sanctuary yet, Sara freezes. Sara's breaths constrict, and her hands clench while her eyes remain trained on the Goddess's encased space. However, she eventually allows her eyes to pull away and take in the rest of her surroundings. She stands in the center of the Goddess's followers' designated living area and stops. Complete with tents and many men, women, and children. Sara's eyes soon rest on a young Brazilian boy and a woman Sara presumes is his mother.

However, Sara finds herself momentarily stuck on the woman and her child as she would have expected the Great Goddess's minions to be older, more worn down, and exposed to what the Goddess does. Yet, these people give Sara the impression that they were born into this crazed world, not brought into it like she knows Charles was as a younger man. Once Sara realizes she has been staring, she notes how the boy and his mother stare back at Sara.

Although this in itself is innocent, it is how they do it that instantly sends shivers down Sara's spine. They look deeply at her as though they already know her, as though they have already met and were waiting for her to return.

Despite the sudden rush of terror that has completely taken her over and the empty pit within her stomach, Sara attempts to break the ice with this pair. She raises a hand and softly waves at the small boy and the seemingly lovely woman, not expecting anything from this small and awkward encounter. However, she is happily proven wrong as they return the wave before setting off. Sara smiles softly, letting it slowly stretch across her face. It had been one of the few moments that had brought her a sliver of happiness and a sense of normality in recent days. It gives her hope that not everything surrounding this place and the Goddess is as bad as the impression she had received. Perhaps there is more than she has seen, what she has encountered.

The Goddess watches Sara interacting with some of her following, noting that Sara has eased up slightly. It offers the Goddess a chance to approach. Yet, she still finds herself cautious. More because of what happened on Mr. Davenport's feeder ship. She must speak softly to Sara, not wanting to put her off anymore.

"They like you," the Goddess gently whispers from behind.

Sara turns, focusing in on the Goddess and noticing how she has begun to carry herself since returning to her home. She appears taller, prouder, and at strength while seeming stripped of the intense energy that the power tends to emanate. She appears to resemble the woman that Sara was fortunate to meet. Although, Sara does her best to ignore the softer and seemingly kinder woman. However, Sara cannot help but dwell on the Great One's glowing sense of power. Noting that the woman holds onto these abilities while not being controlled by the driving force hidden behind the raw power itself.

Yet, Sara does not appear surprised that the Goddess's abilities have heightened. Once stepping onto this soil, she noted how their location impacts their abilities and strengths. Her only concern is the looming threat of the Goddess's temperament and exposure.

"They don't even know me," Sara finally dismisses.

The Goddess considers what Sara said, thinking it over. However, it does not take the Goddess long to move past her curiosity. The Goddess believes she has this in common with Sara. It can bring them together and give Sara perspective. It could be something to soothe her.

"Yes. Well, I think it will interest you to know that they do not know me either. They are aware of my given abilities, what I have accomplished in my rein, what I have given, and my dedication to the role," the Goddess attempts to clarify. "Although, they still do not know me.... I think that Charles is the only one that can come close. It was never any different in the past. No one quite came close enough to understand me. As someone like you, I am sure you know what I mean by this."

Sara pauses, realizing that the Goddess is correct. There are not many people that have ever known Sara. The only exception is her late father and runaway sister. Neither one can be there for her, to know her any longer. This thought instantly causes Sara's eyes to water for emotional torment. Although she does not wish to let the Goddess see her break, she does not permit it. Not now, not when she needs to be strong, when she must be together and ready for what the Goddess has planned.

"Maybe," Sara soon breathes.

While she attempts to hide her agony from the Great One, the Goddess can still undoubtedly note the cold crisp of Sara's voice and inconsistent fluttering of the chest. It alerts the Goddess to Sara's emotional state and currently reserved nature. She must try to correct it before she loses her chance with Sara. The Goddess cannot let Sara get away or not believe in what they are doing here.

"Come with me, will you?" the Goddess asks as she approaches Sara and lightly pulls on her arm, directing her how the Goddess wants. "There is something I would like to show you. Something I believe that you need to see for yourself."

Though Sara finds herself debating whether or not this would be wise, she ultimately decides to follow the Goddess. Whatever the Goddess intends to reveal to her will be nothing compared to what Sara had witnessed and experienced firsthand on board the cargo ship. As Sara follows the Goddess without resistance, the Great One soon releases her grasp on Sara's arm. Yet, they find themselves in silence as they gradually walk through the vast and seemingly endless trenches. However, the awkwardness soon becomes too much for Sara to handle. She does not need another reason to be on edge. Not when they are so close to the end, and Sara still has no idea what her part is in the impending climax. She does not know if she should trust the Goddess and Charles or side with Mr. Davenport's points.

"Where are we going?" Sara asks as she becomes impatient.

A brief and faint smile crosses the Goddess's face before she quickly reclaims her usually collected state. The Great One, however, ignores Sara's query, continuing on her set path and moving long veins and various other plants out of her way. Yet, it appears she will not have to answer as they slowly approach an old and worn structure. Not that it is quite a structure anymore. It was an accent temple, abandoned and left to collapse through the years.

"What is this place?" Sara questions in amazement, eyes fixed on what she naturally assumes to be centuries-old architecture.

The Goddess lets Sara appreciate their surrounding before saying anything. Sara must take everything in before the Goddess explains anything to her. It will help Sara understand more once she connects with it.

"Where many women were brought into power.... Over the years, we were to return to our original location, to the birthplace of the title and power of Mother Nature. This place has been battered and tested beyond what many have ever seen. It is where I go to think, where I first met Charles, and where I informed him of many important matters. It is the closest thing I have to a home," the Goddess reveals. "Hopefully, where you can call your home too."

Sara continues to take in everything that surrounds her, down to the markings and symbols that decorate the entrance to this temple. Almost Egyptian, but not quite. It is something equally beautiful and mysterious. The information is just out of reach. Yet, they all appear to depict a woman of power, just like the Goddess.

However, Sara notices that other images reveal two women posited before a green glow. Yet, she cannot make of any of this. She cannot see anything other than the thick dirt that has made its way over the stone and the trees that grow within the walls of this crumpled empire.

"I don't know if I want it," Sara surprisingly announces to the Goddess.

The woman pauses, unsure what Sara means by this statement, but knows the anxiety that Sara must be going through. It is more than understandable to fear the unknown and a responsibility far greater than anything you have encountered before.

"Would that be the temple or worshipers.... Or even the power in itself?" the Goddess asks purely for clarification, wanting nothing more than to be there for Sara.

Sara looks the woman in the eye, thinking about how to continue without causing an issue for herself and everyone affected by the lack of imbalance and the uncertain future that comes with the multiple ways to change it. Although, Sara does not find many options to work with. Anything could set off the Goddess or change how she perceives Sara's stance.

"All of it," Sara states. "After everything you've done, the connection that you have with whatever controls the power.... You're not even yourself anymore. No life. You have no one anymore, not really. You've said that no one knows you. Just you've done. I mean, I don't even know your name. Does anyone?"

The Goddess stares at Sara, hearing what she has had to say. However, the lack of communication leaves Sara nervous and unsure if she has crossed a line or ruined things for everyone and their chance to live. However, Sara is thankful as the Great One appears to soften.

"Angelina," the Goddess whispers so softly Sara does not catch it.

Sara waits to see if she will repeat herself. However, it does not appear likely. The woman seems withdrawn and ashamed. There is something else here within Sara's reach. It is something that could allow Sara to accept the madness around her.

"Sorry?" she says, realizing that the Goddess is more herself than she has been since meeting Sara.

Yet, the woman appears to struggle with it a great deal. She turns her head away from Sara as if it protects her. However, they know it is useless. The woman will struggle either way. The only difference is what the woman will do now.

"My name, it is Angelina," she repeats. "I told Charles.... He is the only other one who knows."

"It's beautiful," Sara compliments.

They fall silent, taking their time to recompose themselves after this brief moment of humanity they have been given. However, things soon become more awkward between them as neither acknowledges that they are experiencing the bubbling within their chests that usually comes with their abilities. They allow their eyes to rest on each other as if they can speak to each other in this manner.

"I'm not the only one that can feel that, am I?" Sara eventually asks.

There is a silence between them. It is hard enough to be seated across from each other, but it is another to admit anything, no matter how benign or crazy. However, this is different. Whatever is said next will influence Sara's decisions more than anything else.

"No," Angelina cements.

Sara nods despite being aware of this. She turns and notes the long wall of tiles that each appears to reflect the full capability a Goddess in power would possess. As she stays stuck on these tiles for a significant amount of time, Angelina turns and notes what her eyes have become glued to.

"They are fascinating, are they not?" she asks.

"They are. All of this is fascinating, beautiful, and whimsical. But that's not why we're here, is it?" Sara bounces back, understanding what the empathic and intuitive sensation led her to. "What do they mean?"

The Goddess falls silent again, realizing Sara is further along than she expected and has more power and empathic capabilities than she thought. However, Angelina also knows she will not get anywhere with Sara unless she can speak to her.

With this, Angelina approaches the wall, knowing Sara will not be far behind. Once they reach the long and worn line of images, Angelina lifts her hand to the nearest tile and frees it from the thick layer of grime, granting Sara the ability to see the depiction. She sees worshipers bowing down to a woman with dark hair, a Goddess in the seat of power. Yet, Sara does not understand the darkness that encases some images and the unearthly green glow surrounding others. They scream something to her, something that leaves her to take several steps back before finding another tile with two women positioned in the center, encased green glow.

"Most of these have been played out in one way or another. They tell a story. The first Goddess and the destruction of her empire...." Angelina explained per Sara's request. "While others, on the other hand, tell a story.... Though, they are yet to unfold."

Sara momentarily pulls her attention away from the tiles and looks with her overly weary hazel eyes at Angelina to find out whether or not this woman is speaking the truth. However, once Sara spots the expression on her face, Sara knows this to be true. Some of these tiles are clairvoyant.

"Right.... Right," Sara puffs. "And, what's— What's this one?"

Angelina steps closer to see which one Sara means, to see the one Sara seems almost desperate to know. However, as Angelina realizes which image Sara is referring to, she slows. She did not think Sara would stop at and ask about this one so soon.

"That one.... That one in particular is you and I," the Goddess divulges. "We are believed to combine our abilities.... A prime point of power which will bring balance back to this world."

CHAPTER EIGHTEEN

Sara's face loses all color. She is in denial. Not wanting to believe the impossible, what is supposed to be impossible. Sara shakes her head and takes multiple steps back. She nearly trips over backward on the fragmented structure. However, she manages to stay upright.

As the surprise of Angelina's statement wears off, Sara starts to kick herself. She believes she should have seen this coming, that this made more sense than she first thought. Angelina and those that surround her must have gotten this information from somewhere. Charles needed to have something to know that Sara was the one he was searching for.

With this thought, Sara finally permits herself to look at Angelina. However, it appears that Sara is still unable to say anything. She stares at Angelina with her mouth open, trying to let something, anything. Unfortunately, her throat comes to ache from the lack of moisture. Yet, it pales in comparison to Sara's trembling hand.

While Angelina had been watching Sara struggle to deal with the news of the prophecy, the erratic movement in her eyes. It leaves her to worry on Sara's behalf. She knows more than anyone what it is like to deal with influencing news, whether or not it is by choice. The power that presses down upon her at every turn. Always present and the first thought on mind.

"I apologize.... I thought— Was that too much for you to handle? I thought that you would appreciate my honesty. Especially given the weight of what you will endure," Angelina says. "Perhaps.... I could have told you another way."

Sara does not answer. Her attention remains on the tiles, trying to understand what Angelina has said. Yet, it does seem to be working. Sara is unsure, confused, and now unable to look Angelina in the eye. She cannot find anything in the constant and stable through this mess. It makes Sara crazy and unlike herself. She once loved everyone's company, but now Sara does not know who to talk to and who she can trust.

Yet, Sara is grateful that Angelina has shared this with her. Sara has received some honesty from her. It is something Sara has been fighting for. However, she did not expect things to turn out this way. Sara did not believe she would be responsible for so many lives and the world, but here she is.

"No.... I-I— It's okay, I needed to.... I need to know," Sara dismisses.

Angelina and Sara wait in silence for a beat, allowing Sara the chance to collect herself. However, it sadly takes longer than they would have thought. Longer than they would have wished. Sara's breaths gradually returned, allowing her hands to settle.

Once she thinks that she has fully controlled herself, she lifts her attention back to Angelina. Their eyes remain locked for a moment before Sara finally nods. Although, this is not a signal for Angelina. It is more a form of self-confidence. It is something Sara is using to try to convince herself to continue. To keep herself put and to hear Angelina out.

"Alright," Angelina whispers as she steps toward the tiles. "It may be wise to start at the beginning, give you a chance to take in a more.... Reduced manner."

Sara does not respond to this in a hurry. She knows that Angelina is correct in her immediate assumption. Although Sara cannot help but think that things are becoming more prominent, and unfortunately, they all appear to be imminent. Yet, Sara still steps forward, soon standing beside Angelina and politely waiting for an explanation of their designated roles made a millennia ago.

"This is the first known Goddess.... The original and the most powerful," Angelina states while revealing a fading depiction of a beautiful and mighty force. "Though, I might add that there is speculation that there was another.... Another that would have the capability similar to, if not more powerful."

Sara's eyes pull away from the image of the Goddess and look at Angelina, watching as she continues to speak. She notices how Angelina appears lost in the story that she relays. As if it meant more to her than she had stated.

"And this Goddess.... she was the basis to all that ruled in her wake. A prime example. All that she stood for, all that she accomplished, and what she wanted for this world lived through all the women that came after."

As Angelina takes a breath, Sara removes her sight from Angelina to lean forward and get a better look at the woman shown in the image. She notices that this woman looks eerily familiar. She appears to be the woman at Sara's side. Although, Sara cannot think this to be so. Not after everything.

"She would pass down her gift to the next, guide them, and work to preserve the process," Angelina continues. "Although, it was rumored that this woman soon gave a prophecy once the successor proved to be.... How shall I put this? Ill-conceived and disappointing."

Sara takes a moment to note the weight of this statement. To hear what it is that Angelina had said. Yet, it does not change how Sara interpreted it or if she cannot quite grasp why the successor would disappoint the former Goddess.

"How was she disappointing? She was taught by the Goddess, giving the same abilities, and worked for the same cause," Sara points out. "I don't think that I understand."

Angelina falls silent, considering how to answer Sara's reasonable question. However, it does not appear as though she knows how to respond. Not at the moment. Her face and everything about her is reserved, more than usual.

While she expects this from Angelina, Sara still worries about this lack of communication, even more so since they continue to draw closer to Sara's time of supposed enlightenment. It can threaten everything Charles, Mr. Davenport, and Angelina have tried warning her of. Yet, Sara still waits for Angelina to feed her the tiniest bits of information.

"Angelina?" Sara tries. "Did you hear me?"

"Of course," Angelina begins. "I was only wondering how to tell you of such things.... Things I do not believe you will fully understand. Not quite yet. Not until after...."

Sara pauses, thinking Angelina would continue. However, Sara watches Angelina drag this moment out into infinity. It tears Sara apart. She cannot keep going like this, and at the same time, Sara knows she cannot change a thing.

"After what?" Sara questions, sensing a lingering threat from whatever Angelina is dancing around.

Though, Angelina does not answer. Angelina does not know how to tell Sara something this drastic and equally terrible. She continues to leave her statement up to Sara's interpretation, no matter what that may be.

Sara's chest flutters, fearing the worst in this situation. Worrying that she will not be able to contribute to whatever she must endure. What she knows she must accomplish in little time. Her hands tremble again. More powerful than it was before. Although, she does not notice due to the heavy sweat dripping from her fingertips. She attempts to wipe them free of the moisture. However, she fails. It is too thick, and she gets distracted by the shiver running down her spine.

The terror continues to expel and wears off on Angelina. It fills her face with a strange expression that Sara has not seen her pull since their encounter. Perhaps the first real sign of humanity Sara has seen. The woman beneath the power that has its hold over her. However, it does not stay long. It leaves Angelina's face faster than it had manifested. Yet, Sara does not seem to mind. It offers a glimmer of hope that she will reach Angelina, not the person who was exposed to the outside world for years.

"After our.... Conjoined efforts, our partnership reveals the truth to you," Angelina eventually replies. "Perhaps I should continue at a slower pace. Tell you of the things that you wish to know from the beginning. Starting with the Goddess and what came from her. The rest will follow naturally."

"Alright," Sara agrees.

Angelina takes this moment to review what she has already revealed and consider what she could continue to divulge. Allowing Sara into the world she believes she is a part of while keeping her further away from things Sara must not know yet. Yet, Angelina's train of thought constantly drifts with the power that can control her becoming present. It forces her line of sight to occasionally gaze toward where the routine will happen.

The influencing voice at the base of her skull continues to pressure Angelina into escorting Sara to the open space. The thing is far from a haven at this point. However, Angelina presses past the drowning sensation. She will continue to find a way to stall her and reveal things she will hopefully understand.

"The prophecy stated that *power will escalate. Growing stronger with each woman fit for reign. Bring forth one that will liberate while charging and effecting another seated in a prime position of power,*" Angelina enlightens. "This was passed through the years, what it could truly mean.... Is perhaps lost on most."

"What do you think it means?" Sara asks, wanting to get her opinion.

Angelina thinks about this, wondering how to tell Sara. However, there are not many options. The only thing she can think of requires soft stepping around the truth.

"Well.... I think that it means we must work together. That our combined power will be like anything anyone has seen," Angelina states.

Sara soon finds herself silent, stewing on the fresh information she has, thinking about this apparent prophecy that a Goddess had set into motion. Though, she does not seem to have much of a reaction to the news, perhaps expecting it due to the craziness that has unfolded in recent days. It could also be because she stands beside Mother Nature, knowing she must take over the role and maintain the Earth's stability.

"And what happened to the Goddess? To the both of them," Sara questions.

Angelina considers this question. However, she soon permits herself to answer Sara with a partial truth. Angelina believes that this piece of information will serve them well. Not to mention that she will be putting off this transaction between them for a while longer.

"The original Goddess, the one that bestowed her centuries-long wisdom upon the other.... She went on to reclaim her title and continued to work for the better of life until it came time to perform another ritual. Pass the title down to another and double the power," Angelina answers as she watches Sara.

However, Sara does not give Angelina anything to work with. The better part of her has learned from the Goddess. She is quiet and almost stone-like, with her facial queues and breathing somewhat reserved and not offering insight into what could run inside her mind.

"What happens after?" Sara eventually asks, needing to know.

"I am.... I am not entirely sure what you mean," Angelina states.

Sara cannot find words that express what she is trying to convey. Not for now, at least. Not with everything that she has had to acknowledge.

However, Sara soon turns to the tiles, thinking they will help influence her in the following. Help Sara form what only lies on her mind. Her eyes rest on the image of what she assumes to be the two of them, Sara and Angelina, floating in the green mist. Allowing her this slim chance to correctly collect herself and find a way to ask things she is unsure of.

"We're doing this because of what this Goddess predicted, yes? We will combine our power to bring balance and whatever else, right? But I don't know how. How do we plan to do that, and what will come of it? The consequences that will follow," Sara begins. "There are consequences for everything.... And everyone. Who will end up paying for this?"

Angelina stops to almost hear what Sara is trying to warn her of. Yet, it means nothing to her. She brushes past this. However, it is not due to her lack of empathy for Sara or understanding. It is because of the overwhelming sense of her ability beginning to drown out the woman inside again.

The power soon persuades Angelina to look at Sara the way she had the first time she encountered Sara. As something of great potential, not the person she knows Sara is. Leaving Angelina to slowly turn her attention back toward where she must bring Sara. To where everything began and will ultimately end.

"Well, in all honesty.... May I call you Sara?" Angelina asks.

Sara nods quickly, not wanting to drag things out unnecessarily. Not now of all time.

"If I am to be honest with you, Sara, you have no experience or training for such an extreme situation as I have. You will act as a battery for myself," the Goddess reveals. "As you may have already noticed, my power is already remarkable. The combined efforts of all energy that came to pass before. With the addition of your new and truly heightened ability. There will be almost no end to what I can accomplish."

Sara stares at the Goddess. She is stuck on the fact that she will not be the one to bring about a stage of enlightenment but will be an advanced form of battery for someone she cannot trust.

Sara combs through what the Goddess has revealed and believes she may have found the reasoning behind what the Goddess wishes to achieve. It terrifies Sara to her core. And not for herself.

"You do mean *what we can accomplish,* don't you?" Sara questions more to pull the Goddess's attention, to capture the sharpness inside.

Something suddenly clicks behind the Goddess's eyes. It leaves Sara to smile, knowing that she has indeed triggered deeper. However, neither one of them acknowledges this. They choose to move forward with their current conversation because of their impending situation.

"Of course," she states.

While neither one believes this, they both turn toward the Goddess's home, to the camping site. They feel the sudden pull of their power beginning to gnaw away at them. It calls them in, persuading them to finish what is in motion. Yet, they both seem equally hesitant and fearful.

"We should go," the Goddess announces.

Sara looks the Goddess in the eye, considering leaving all this behind one last time. Although, she knows that she mustn't and that everything that has happened to Sara has led her to this moment. That she and whatever ability she possesses will influence what will take place tonight, hopefully, for the better.

"Yes.... I think you're right. We should get going," Sara replies.

She and the Goddess step away from the abandoned temple, watching out for snaking roots and broken bits of stone along the way. Walking in silence, not knowing how to approach either other in the wake of what they are about to undertake. Though, Sara finds herself thankful for this moment of solitude. It gives her time to think over and move past most mental roadblocks that present a problem for her.

Yet, it does not prevent Sara from trying to find a way to free her from this inconvenient predicament. From what she can only assume to be a harrowing and draining experience. Although, somehow, she cannot see herself abandoning Angelina. Especially as she notes the overwhelming sense that has its hold over Angelina. It calls to her, forcing Angelina to do its bidding, burying the woman inside to create a Goddess.

Sara must help her. She must find a way to save the lives of people she has never met and never will. She has to become a Goddess, whatever capacity that may be, for all that needs her help.

As they continue to make their way through the rainforest, Sara takes in the scenery. It offers her a chance to distance herself from another awkward conversation with the Goddess while she attempts to think of a way to correct everything. Especially now, given that the Goddess has indirectly admitted her intentions to Sara. However, it does not appear like the Goddess has the same thoughts regarding their short-distance travel.

"Are you quite nervous?" the Goddess asks.

Sara turns to the Goddess, wanting to watch her reaction as she answers, no matter the bitterness.

"Yes and no…. It's like I've been waiting for this, and it's now here," Sara replies. "I think now I'm just waiting to get back there."

The Goddess's expression does not change. However, with Sara's heightened power on the Amazon, she notes the Goddess's quickened pulse and oddly slowed breaths. Offering Sara a great insight into what she may be dealing with once she steps into whatever the Goddess will have in store for her.

"That is good to hear," the Goddess says without emotional context.

Once the uncomfortable and dreaded conversation between herself and the Goddess finally dies, Sara looks up to believe they are almost back at the campsite. Not far from the Goddess's sanctuary. Not far from where everything will both end and begin.

She lets out a soft breath, perhaps a sigh. Though it had lost all its momentum as it left her mouth. Maybe caught in agony. Noticing the fact that the space before her both calls to her and warns her. Telling her to maintain her distance from everything she fears. Although, Sara continues with her head higher than she would have thought.

As Sara and the Goddess draw closer to the Goddess's sanctuary, Sara slows. Not from fear of or for herself, she nearly stops because of the overwhelming tightening of her chest. A feeling that Sara has only felt on a handful of occasions. A sensation that gives them some of the direst warnings that she may hear. Sara remains alert before stepping into the unknown with the Goddess, searching for anything to explain this dreaded sensation.

However, it does not take long to find the cause. Sara's sight remains frozen, fixed on Charles and his familiar form as it zooms through the forestation. She stops moving, wanting to know what or whom he is searching for. Yet, she soon sees that he appears to be running from another. A worn and almost destroyed Mr. Davenport ran after him with a crazed look in his eye.

CHAPTER NINETEEN

Sara steps away from the Goddess, wanting to go after Charles and Mr. Davenport. She wonders if Charles is alright after his incident on Mr. Davenport's feeder ship. Sara wants to know what has transpired since their last encounter. However, the Goddess has other plans. She throws her arm out, blocking Sara. It forces Sara's body to collide with the Goddess's surprisingly sturdy arms before they dig their eyes into each other. Sara wants to help those in their immediate vicinity, but the Goddess only thinks about the goals from hundreds of years prior.

"What are you doing?" Sara questions.

The Goddess appears taken aback. She did not think Sara would react like this. Not when everything, goals, time, and Earthly planes were so close. The Goddess believed Sara would have seen what she was trying to do. However, she is disappointed and aggravated.

"What are you doing?" the Goddess redirects. "You know what we must do. They are two grown men. Men who know what this moment means. They can deal with their problems."

Sara stares at the Goddess, considering this. On one hand, she believes Charles and Mr. Davenport need assistance. On the other, the better part of humanity needs Sara's attention. She soon realizes the Goddess is correct and that she must push past all distractions. No matter what they may be or the weight of them.

Sara's shoulders relax before she nods, letting the Goddess know she will cooperate with the process. More because this is the only thing she can do. Not after realizing her mistake and knowing many will suffer. She must be willing to do whatever it takes.

The Goddess drops her arm and pulls it away. Yet, she is still cautious that Sara will not keep her word. However, the Goddess's action grants them enough space to move. It lets them breathe and have a chance to relax.

While it seems unlikely to relax, Sara and the Goddess try to ease around each other. Once they are comfortable with one another again, they step forward, coming to enter the Goddess's circler, meditation space. It is her designated work space and where the power will be whole.

Sara's attention lifts toward the beautiful light beams leaking through the intertwined vines and tree branches. It gives Sara a moment of bliss and an alluring vision. However, it proves to be short as she needs to force herself to note how everything has spiraled in and around where she knows the Goddess works. Everything circles the slightly off-centered honey-colored pillar. The Thorne scares Sara to her core.

"It's beautiful," Sara states.

"Yes.... It is, Isn't it?" the Goddess says, looking around. "I do not believe I notice anymore."

Sara is surprised. She would have thought that Mother Nature would appreciate the greenery around her. The Amazon alone is breathtaking and gorgeous. However, the Goddess's assigned workspace looks like it belongs in a fairytale.

"No?" Sara questions.

The Goddess allows her focus to land on Sara. However, she does not speak. The Goddess struggles with a thought and considers what she can divulge. Cautious of the looming ability that presses down upon her.

"No," the Goddess confirms. "I tend to get a little caught in my work.... For the Earth's better part, of course."

Sara does not know what she thought the Goddess would say. Yet, she is still disappointed and feels regret and shame rising from her stomach. Sara knows what is supposed to happen next. However, it does not make things any easier.

"Right," Sara puffs.

She pulls away from the Goddess, knowing that this conversation between herself and the Goddess will be their last in a while. Sara fears the looming threat of the transaction in the coming moments. She knows there is nothing left standing in their way.

"Should we get to it?" the Goddess asks as if she could read Sara's mind.

Sara's pulse quickens again, dreading the unknown that is about to take place. And having her fear violently burrow in the base of her stomach, painfully wrapping around her torso, a tight bear hug restricting her ability to breathe. However, Sara pushes herself to look up at the Goddess and nod her head. Unable to speak. Yet, she cannot pull her attention away from the Goddess.

"Good," the Goddess states.

Sara watches as the Great Goddess walks toward the pillar that sits slightly off-center and takes a seat. However, Sara cannot help but feel inferior and useless, unsure how to proceed. She stands like a fool. Yet, it does not last long. The Goddess extends her hand, indicating the space before her, wanting Sara to join her in this crazed ordeal. She wants to bring about everything she has worked for.

"Come, sit. Please," the Goddess says.

Sara looks at her, worried about whatever the outcome may be. However, she ultimately steps forward and places herself at least three feet from the Goddess, waiting for the process to begin. Yet, Sara still does not feel comfortable about the mystical procedure.

"What now?" Sara asks.

The Goddess smiles, sending shivers down Sara's spine. However, it does not appear to be of an evil purpose, perhaps finding some humor in this situation. Yet, it still puts Sara at odds with this act. Especially as it seems misplaced on the Goddess's face, leaving Sara unsure how to respond, not that she needs to. Not with the Goddess caught in the mess that is the transition.

"You will close your eyes.... As I have the majority of the power, I will control how it moves and how to use it," the Goddess reveals. "You will be present. However, you cannot intervene with the following. You will have no control over the power coursing through us."

While Sara is aware of everything happening to her and the excitement emanating from the Goddess, Sara feels empty. Everything that was once her has vanished and left her with nothing more than a husk. The odd sensation worries Sara. Yet, she does not think much of it. Her mind is elsewhere, trained on what is unfolding.

"Sounds thrilling," Sara states, finally able to speak.

However, she knows the real reason she cannot be honest with herself and the Goddess is because of the fear she holds. It forces her to allow sarcastic comments to roll off her tongue in hopes of misleading the Goddess. More because she knows of the capabilities the Goddess can achieve.

"Should I expect anything?" Sara questions, pulling herself away from her occasionally sarcastic self, knowing there must be something to validate her terror.

However, Sara briefly wonders whether or not the real reason she questions the Goddess is because she wants to push things out. Sara puts off the transition a bit longer, not wanting to give in to this craziness.

"Yes.... A whirlwind," the Goddess answers.

Sara pauses, unsure what the Goddess meant by this statement. However, she will find out and see it firsthand. The Goddess's eyes close, and Sara feels compelled to do the same. Yet, she cannot. Sara has this lingering need to watch what happens.

Yet, she still has the urge as wisps of air suddenly encircle them. It encases them in the small and somewhat closed-off area. The abrupt gusts of wind bring in a familiar green mist that swirls near Sara and curls toward her fingertips. She lifts her hand, fearing the unnaturally colorful cloud. However, Sara realizes she must trust whatever comes through this space and the process involved. Her hand reaches forward, trying to touch whatever this strange fog is.

Once Sara comes into contact with the substance, her head whips back, and her body gets thrust into the air. At this moment of uncertainty and terror, Sara is too surprised and frightened to scream. She can only look down at the Goddess, hoping the woman inside knows what she is doing.

The Goddess lifts in the same manner as Sara. Yet, she does it more elegantly. Her arms extend, head tilted back as her body meets Sara's, barely inches apart. It is enough for Sara to reach out and touch the Goddess if she wants. However, Sara does not. She has become too lost in the literal gripping situation. Afraid that she will not touch the ground.

The Goddess's eyes suddenly open, revealing that her eyes appear to have taken on some of the glow from the surrounding mist. These growling green eyes fixate on Sara, locking into hers. Almost as if there were something she was trying to read from Sara. Yet, this does not seem to be the case. The Goddess seems caught in the power that flows through her. However, it is nothing compared to what they know she will wield in the coming moments. It fills Sara with an uneasy sensation before the green mist swirls around them, trapping them in an unfortunate colored wind funnel.

Before Sara can understand what is happening, the cloud disappears despite the drastic events that have led to it. Yet, Sara looks about, trying to find where it may have gotten to. Her eyes rest on the last ruminates of the green haze that traces her hands. It almost follows them as she moves them about, attempting to rid it.

"Give me your hands," the Goddess demands, bringing Sara out of her obscure moment.

Though she is skeptical about what the Goddess has planned, Sara's hands go out to the Goddess. They quickly intertwine, allowing an immense surge of power between them. Such energy suddenly pulses through the enclosed space. For a moment, Sara's mind fills with nothing except clarity.

However, it gets ripped from her with all the air in her lungs. She gags from the lack of oxygen and notes how her brain aches like someone squeezes it. The restriction alone would have sent stress through Sara's body instantly. Yet, she cannot respond.

Sara quickly realizes that she cannot do anything except float, momentarily flailing about, unsure of what could remedy the situation, not knowing anything she could do to save herself. Thinking that she has already lost her right to be, Sara is distracted by the unexpected darkness that washes over them. However, Sara can no longer find distractions in her surroundings nor comprehend what she is undergoing. Her life's essence is slipping away.

"Angelina!" a familiar male voice screams from the ground below.

The Great Goddess chooses to ignore that the sky has gone dark and the voice that calls to her at first. Especially as the moment she had been waiting for had finally arrived. Next to nothing was going to stop her now. However, something bothers her. Slowly drilling into her mind and telling her something more significant was happening than she knew.

"Angelina!" the voice screams again.

Nothing happens. Everything is silent. The Goddess does not let this voice get the better of her. She does not want to give up everything she has worked for. Yet, the Goddess knows this voice may still interfere.

"Miss Bronstein!" another shouts.

The Goddess turns her attention downwards, focusing on Charles and Mr. Davenport, noting their wagered expressions and general essence. Yet, it does not appear to be something that bothers the Goddess. Not once does her eyes lock into Charles's.

What seems to be hope momentarily expels from her, wanting to remain between them. However, the Goddess returns to her more indoctrinated state, and she is glad he is okay. She was worried Charles may have been permanently affected by the events on Mr. Davenport's ship.

Yet, the power surging through the Goddess's veins causes another gush of emotionlessness to cut her off from what lies before her. Sara turns her attention and the full load of her ability to the task at hand. She still seeps energy and power for the Goddess, shaping the world.

"Miss Bronstein!" Mr. Davenport yells harder than he had before. "Miss Bronstein! Look at me!"

Despite being barely conscious, Sara managed to hear Mr. Davenport's call. However, turning her line of sight to him proves to be almost impossible. Her eyes are glued shut as her life hangs by a thread. As it is, Sara struggles to get slivers of air between bursts of energy that pour from her and the Goddess.

"Miss Bronstein, you need to look at me! You can stop all this!" he attempts.

He hopes this will reach her and Sara will free herself from this madness. Yet, Mr. Davenport faces the reality that she may not free herself from the Goddess's hold. The Goddess might be too powerful.

Unfortunately, it soon shows that she cannot separate herself from her overwhelming power in this state of heightened ability. Yet, this crippling fact does not stop either Mr. Davenport or Charles from trying to reach Billie and the Goddess. They must talk some rationality into the woman Charles wants to be in there. Something human. Free Sara from her infliction and what will unfortunately be her end.

"Angelina.... You need to let her breathe!" Charles tries. "You're killing them.... You're killing her like all the others. You told me you didn't want to do it. So, don't. Let Sara go, let her breathe!"

Yet, it does not appear like the Goddess is listening to reason. She continues her work, focused on Sara. It is almost like they had not spoken. As Charles and Mr. Davenport's hopes fade, the light they could see through the swirling ducks of air quenches. It leaves everyone in complete and utter darkness. Unsure of what takes place before them.

However, they are soon enlightened about what the Goddess is up to. The air turns cold and seems to thrust toward the sky, pulling everything near Sara and the Goddess with the gust of wind. The Goddess enacts her plan, forcing the power around to do her bidding.

Thunder rumbles off in the distance, and the ground beneath their feet trembles uncontrollably. Almost threatening to tear apart the Earth's seems. It fills Charles with more fear than he knew possible. Especially as he knows what is happening, knowing that this Earth-bending feat is worldwide. A purge of anything that the Goddess does not deem pure. Men and women alike. The likings of Mr. Davenport included.

"Angelina! Please! It's me!" Charles screams. "You need to stop. You can save her, you can save Sara. You can save yourself!"

As if she could sense what was happening around her, Sara's body jerked. Yet, her mind appears to be numb and caught in nothingness. A sensation that she cannot say she enjoys. It hurts Sara, wearing her down.

However, she does not seem alone in this extreme mental state. Sara finds herself trapped alongside Angelina. Floating in a familiar green mist that she had witnessed swarm around her. Unfortunately, no one appears to be up to having a conversation, not in their exhausted and strained condition. They fight for their right to stay conscious, to stay alive.

Yet, with determination and people counting on her, Sara continues to try. Simply trying to move, speak, and navigate this strange and isolating dimension, trying to reach Angelina. Reach the woman held captive by the power that comes from them, the power destroying life.

Luckily, little by little, Sara slowly pushes forward and finds her way to Angelina. Beginning by wiggling her fingers, then her toes. Soon, Sara can move on to her limbs. Once she can finally move freely, Sara heads to Angelina, attempting to gather her attention.

Although, this proves to be a problem. Tears have engulfed her face, and Angelina is in an almost catatonic state. Unable to move, waiting to be freed. Yet, this is sadly a state that Angelina has known for a long time. She knows how to be stuck in oblivion.

"An— Angelina," Sara struggles to whisper.

However, Angelina does not turn or move in the slightest. Yet Sara can tell from looking into her eyes that Angelina can hear her, revealing that Angelina is still within her reach. She can still get saved from this nightmare that affected them for too long.

Knowing that she could save Angelina, Sara puts a hand on Angelina's, hoping the contact and affection will in some way aid the situation. Help reach Angelina. Yet, she does not know how much this simple action could help because of the power that has controlled her for hundreds of years.

"Angelina.... I know what it's like. The power— It talks to you. It overwhelms you, trying to get you to do things. Things you don't want and that you know you can't do," Sara begins. "It's worn you down over the years, become too powerful for you to handle anymore."

Angelina's eyes flicker, giving Sara a faint sign of life. It offers them some satisfaction, showing them that Sara is getting through. She might help Angelina free herself. They could both escape the Goddess.

"I can see what's happening with you and everything else. I know you can too. Why else would you be this distraught? But we can't do anything from here," Sara explains. "What would Charles want you to do? What would you know he would want you to do right now?"

With this, Angelina slowly pulls out of her waking coma, coming to focus on Sara's worried expression. Though, this does not last long. They slip away from this dark and mystical dimension, returning to their unfortunate reality.

Through this dark and serial moment of destruction, Angelina looks down at Charles. Knowing full well of the agony that she undoubtedly put him through. However, it does not appear as though Charles minds. Not after realizing Angelina looks down upon him and not the Goddess lurking behind the curtain. She is no longer in control of the woman he cares for.

With this newfound command over all her functions and decisions, Angelina lets the draining hold over Sara ease. It lets Sara breathe, allowing her to reconnect with Angelina. It brings them a state of ability and control.

CHAPTER TWENTY

Sara and Angelina's eyes meet. They are cautious and somewhat eager as energy runs through their veins. Sensing what they will allow to pass through them causes them to shake. It is like they were moments away from bursting. The power they possess leaves them staring at each other, caught in this terrifying circumstance between them.

Charles also knows what these women can do with their heightened power, seeing them almost dripping with raw power from their link. It leaves Charles to step back, sensing what will take place. He pulls Mr. Davenport along with him. It is well-timed too. Angelina and Sara reach a nonverbal agreement, only communicating with one another through the emotion reflected in their eyes. Their heads tilt back, palms slowly facing outwards, and energy expels from them. It knocks Charles and Mr. Davenport clean off their feet.

However, it does not appear as though Sara and Angelina notice. Not at this moment, at least. Their attention becomes firmly trained on the sky above them. They are attempting to correct the damage that the Goddess had already done and what she had set into motion, trying to settle the rumbling grounds of the Earth. Yet, they both know they cannot correct the casualties the Goddess had already claimed.

However, this unfortunate circumstance does not stop them from trying to stop the domino effect. Try to save those currently falling victim to the Goddess's crazed mess. Luckily, they soon calm the dirt beneath everyone's feet, allowing Sara and Angelina to rest their focus on one another. For a moment, they are blissful, knowing the dangers they had just avoided.

However, they are soon caught in dread and only stare at one another. Unable to do anything else. Aware that they must intervene with another equally dangerous and miserable issue.

The matter of the Earth's declining stability. A subject neither one of them wishes to be stewing on. An issue that no one wishes to be thinking of. Especially as everyone had a role to play in the effect humanity has had on their home planet. Some more than others. Yet, this does not change the fact that this unavoidable event would happen.

Although currently faced with something that appears to have only a few outcomes, many with the death of most, something clicks in Sara's mind. It leaves her to look down at Mr. Davenport with a thought trapped within the construct of her mind.

"Mr. Davenport," Sara says through the troubling mist.

While he finds his footing on the ground again, Davenport struggles with the rushing winds surrounding him. It causes him to take longer to make eye contact with Sara than they would have thought. However, the second he does, he notes the severity of the raw emotion within her eyes.

"I was wrong about you once before because of missing information.... I thought there might be a chance it's the case now," Sara explains. "What your satellite does....? Is it as terrible as I've heard?"

Angelina and Charles give Sara a look of warning, leaving her feeling slightly uncomfortable. To somewhat reel away from knowing they disapprove of the subject matter. However, it does not change the fact that she must know. Everyone depending on her must know.

Yet, her sure attitude momentarily dies. She fills with regret once Sara notes the pause on Mr. Davenport's part. However, this pause does not last long. Mr. Davenport allows his face to twist into a strange and misplaced smile. It eventually becomes a loud chuckle. It leaves Sara and the others in a state of fear. Unsure of his true intentions and what he could be capable of in their vicinity.

"It does what I said it does...... what they've told it does," Mr. Davenport answers. "Because they fail to see that this was a temporary solution. You've been misled."

Charles looks to Mr. Davenport. Something desperate stuck in his eyes, wearing them down. However, Charles does not appear to care that it is there. Not now. Not when he needs Mr. Davenport to hear the weight of what he has to say.

"Mr. Davenport.... Whether this is temporary or not, once you start to mess with the natural order of events. The laws of nature change in ways we cannot predict. Reject all you've done to change what you don't like about it. We'll see drought where you've attempted to bring rain, billiards where you've tried to bright summer," Charles begins. "It will end in chaos.... Worse than what we've seen already."

Everyone stares at Charles for a long beat. Unsure of what to do next. Particularly Sara and Mr. Davenport, unable to bring themselves to look away. Powerless, not knowing how to remedy the situation. Luckily, it becomes clear to Charles that he is the one who has the answer and brings everyone out of this awkward state.

"As stated, the only course of action to take is to.... Restart with a blank slate. Go back to the beginning. Only man will at least have a chance to learn from their mistakes. That's if we can," Charles says. "We need to do a-a reboot.... not like the purge the Goddess personally had put into motion."

Sara pauses, wondering what he could mean by this. Whether his plan would endanger lives, the very lives that the Goddess had intentionally tried to end. Though she cannot fathom the idea of Charles being as chaotic and reckless, Sara cannot put this possibility past him. Not after the years he had spent alongside the Goddess, falling for the woman inside.

"Charles...... What are you suggesting?" Sara asks.

Charles takes a moment to himself, considering the words that threaten to follow. He is deciding whether it is best to inform them of the thought that runs through his mind, knowing that once the words escape his mouth. There will be no turning back. He would either be deemed a savior or the likely savage. However, he realizes that he must discuss this, no matter the consequences. The world is bigger than one person.

"I'm not saying the Goddess was right.... Not with such dire means and destruction," Charles stresses. "I just believe that maybe we could.... Riddle certain areas of the planet useless. Unobtainable."

Though he had not been particularly forthcoming, Angelina and Sara had realized what Charles had been trying to explain. Angelina's eyes linger on his as she nods with kindness and warmth as if thanking him for an opportunity to fix all the wrongs she had unintentionally aided in. It is not to mention that he has stayed by her side through all this insanity. And the love she will always have for him.

However, she soon forces herself to tear her attention away from Charles, lifting it alongside Sara. They resume their more powerful positioning, trying to do as he had suggested.

Yet, this sends the green mist toward Mr. Davenport and Charles. Once again, knocking them to the ground, rolling from the pain.

Yet, the real struggle is between Sara and Angelina. They strain themselves before the power consumes them mentally and emotionally, taxing them more than they would have predicted with their brief experience. It would prove to be too much for most. However, neither Sara nor Angelina are like most. They were built for this very circumstance, this very moment.

However, their consciousness seeps in upon them, disturbing them more than they would admit. More because they know that they will forever change the lives of everyone on the planet and how they live.

Aware that there is a chance that this could eliminate a few people. Yet, this does not change the fact that they must press on. Think of the better part of humanity.

The green cloud spreads outwards, stretching into the depths of humanity. The poor people, Sara's eyes come to rest onto Angelina's as if to reassure them that they are doing the right thing. An encouraging nod from Angelina's part allows Sara to go on, to carry herself just a bit higher and let this green cloud go, settle down upon certain parts of damaged Earth, root beneath it.

It slowly starts causing Earth-moving disasters, destroying areas where she and Angelina know no sane person will be due to the ongoing phenomena. Collapsing mining sites, refreezing melting icecaps. And much more devastation than what they would have initially thought they would have to induce.

It naturally continues for quite a bit longer. Sara and Angelina must take their time, ensuring they do as they promised. However, it drains them beyond what Charles and Mr. Davenport like to bear witness to.

Watching Sara and Angelina's faces sink. Obliged to take in their pale and depleting bodies diminish. Yet, the gentlemen must do nothing more for the time being. There is not much they could do other than the fact. The women are the ones with the connection to the power riddling the Earth victim.

However, Mr. Davenport does not seem enthused with the situation, growing more sickened by every minute. Although, it does not take too long for him to conjure a potentially world-shaking idea. One that he believes will aid the women in their tried efforts. Though, he does not know how he will enlist the help of Charles. Or at least find a way to move past him.

"What are the chances of you helping me set up another one of my satellites?" Mr. Davenport asks boldly.

Charles looks to him, dumbfounded by Mr. Davenport's query. He wonders if he is asking this question when it has already been dismissed.

"You have another one?" Charles questions seriously.

"Of course.... You think I would take the chance when dealing with you and the Goddess?" he points out.

Charles stares at the man before him, questioning what could be running through his calculating mind. However, this does not get him far, not with Mr. Davenport. At this point, he is nothing more than a wild card.

"The whole point of this was so that we didn't destroy the natural ways to the planet and ultimately spare countless lives.... Your plan did just that. It would kill the world and everyone on it," Charles reiterates. "Why would we go out of our way to do just that?"

"Because.... I've isolated the Earth-bending elements present during the Goddess's rein," Mr. Davenport begins. "I can help the girls in their efforts.... Spare their lives."

Charles considers this, trying to decide whether or not to trust Mr. Davenport with the subject. He wonders if Mr. Davenport will save the women from their unfortunate demise or if he will endanger the atmosphere and destroy all they have worked for.

CHARLES STILL HAS RESERVATIONS about Mr. Davenport's ability and suspicions about this plan. However, it soon became clear that the gentlemen needed to aid the women in any way they could. Angelina and Sara are declining at a concerning rate.

Now Charles is trekking through slightly damaged ground in search of Mr. Davenport's setup, wherever it may be in the rainforest. Though, there are only so many places it could be. Charles hopes that he is doing the right thing. However, his attention soon shifts, focusing on Mr. Davenport as they stretch further and further out into the forestation.

So much so that they have wandered back to where they had come from. Closer to the American claim. Their borrowed soil. It leads Charles to assume Mr. Davenport's prized satellite is near his vessel. Closer to where they had witnessed the destruction of the last. To the prebuilt platform that the Americans had always planned on interfering with.

However, Charles cannot complain. Not now. Not when Angelina and Sara need him to come through. Save them from something that has a high probability of killing them. Almost with complete certainty if he were being honest with himself.

They make their way toward where the devastation still lies. It has washed to the shore, sticking out of the beautiful yet distilled water. The mess that unevenly lies charred beside Mr. Davenport's ship, Charles cannot help but let out a breath, becoming as lifeless as the devastation before him.

Yet, Charles manages to push past this and turn his sight to Mr. Davenport, hoping to get a glimpse of his intention. However, Charles only sees pain and ruin. Charles is unsure of how authentic this may be, especially as Mr. Davenport has already admitted that he has another Earth-manipulating device.

It gives Charles the impression that Mr. Davenport wants to do as he sets out. Just waiting. Waiting to launch the hefty device into the atmosphere and affect all that he and the American government wish. More likely for the want of turning over profits than for the better of humanity.

"Alright," Mr. Davenport says once reaching the waterline. "You ready?"

He looks to Charles, wanting an immediate answer. However, it takes a moment longer than he would have thought. Charles seems stuck, doing nothing more than staring into the broken abyss. Almost in search of something out there that could mend the issues within him. Something that could solve all the problems that he has.

Fortunately, Charles has a chance at something close, something to aid him in his pursuit to please Angelina. Save her from her infliction. Though, Mr. Davenport does not view what is happening the same way. He sees it more as an opportunity rather than a solution. Not for gain. To do what his father only wished to do.

"Charles," Mr. Davenport mumbles.

With this, Charles finally collects himself, noticing that Mr. Davenport wishes to move on, trying to edge them forward.

"What do we do?" He questions.

"We swim out," Davenport answers.

Mr. Davenport leads their movement. He goes on to remove his shoes and jump right into the water. Davenport swims toward the devastation. Knowing that Charles will eventually join him, he does not consider looking back.

However, this fades. Worry starts to set in as nothing seems to come to pass. Charles has not blessed Mr. Davenport with his presence in the water, reconsidering what they are doing. Yet, Mr. Davenport is lucky enough to be put at ease. He hears Charles splashing not too far behind.

Thankfully, the swim is not too long. Mr. Davenport and Charles seem pleased, not wanting to face anything that lurks underneath the water or succumb to the dangerous tide. Davenport is the first to reach the fallen platform. He is happy to find that it is stable to stand upon. Yet, he soon turns to watch the water, waiting for Charles to be at his side. Luckily, it does not take Charles much longer. He pulls himself free of the water to survey their surroundings, questioning something.

"Where's the satellite exactly?" Charles cannot help but ask.

"Yeah, Charles.... That's the thing," Davenport begins. "There isn't another one."

Charles's expression hardens, aggravated by the subterfuge. Although, he cannot fully understand the meaning behind it. If Mr. Davenport does not indeed have a satellite, he could not induce the change he had set out to do.

"You said you had another satellite that can project the elements present when the goddess uses her ability," Charles says. "Now you're telling me we have nothing?"

Mr. Davenport smiles, reaching down to the platform and pressing on the metallic floor beneath them before lifting a panel free. He pulls out what appears to be a compartment to reveal a computer-like device. Something that Davenport needed desperately.

Perhaps information that could be of use to him. While Charles is unaware of what it is Mr. Davenport is up to. He cannot do anything but helplessly watch as Mr. Davenport speedily flicks various switches and begins typing something too fast for Charles to register.

It activates something that shifts the ground beneath them. Maneuvering the platform before the somewhat sunken remains of the satellite appear to open. Putting Charles off. Thinking the worst. Fearing for everyone, he steps back, at a loss and unsure what to do.

"What are you doing?" he questions softly.

A wait between them passes, adding to the extreme tension and terror that overruns them. It overwhelms them more than they could bear at the moment. Not on top of everything.

"Projecting the elements the goddess uses when she controls her ability," Mr. Davenport answers. "I was just taking my precautions."

Charles looks again at the machinery, aiming upward as if he could decide whether or not this is the truth with a glance. However, this is not the case. He cannot judge what Mr. Davenport has done with this device, nor why he had decided to rely on disseat. It leaves Charles's attention to drift back to Mr. Davenport.

"Why didn't you just tell me?" Charles wonders.

"Would you have come if I had told you the truth?" Mr. Davenport asks.

Charles pauses for a brief moment, considering the question. However, his expression ultimately relaxes, realizing they already know the truth behind the question.

"Fair point," Charles finally admits.

While the gentlemen find amusement in this statement, the top of this makeshift satellite retracts. It gathers Mr. Davenport's attention. He stares at this unnerving sight as a nozzle slowly exits the device.

Before Davenport can reach Charles, the nozzle expels a green gas. One similar to the mist that engulfed Angelina and Sara. Although, the boys have learned their lesson. They manage to remain standing. However, their stance seems as though they would fall at any moment.

Yet, neither one of them cares at this point. They focus on the cloud still spreading out, heading back to where they had left the girls, leaving Charles and Mr. Davenport to stare at the gas uncontrollably. They wonder if this action has their desired effect, whether or not it will aid Sara and Angelina in their atmosphere-bending trance.

After a short while, Charles and Mr. Davenport unfortunately lose hope, fearing that it had been for nothing. The women will still have to fend for themselves in every way.

However, their opinions ultimately shift.

The mist funnels and heads for the unnaturally colored sky before shooting up above where the women were. It clears outward, moving on before it eventually subsides.

As Mr. Davenport and Charles stand there, unsure of anything, everything settles. The skies return to normal. However, they strangely appear clearer than before they had initially landed.

Charles looks down, seeing that the waters finally rest. It is unlike anything he had seen here since first encountering Angelina and the Goddess. Unlike anything, Angelina could accomplish with the Goddess's untimely interference.

Charles slowly looks at Mr. Davenport, realizing they are coming to the same conclusion. The women must have achieved their goals. They had destroyed man's harmful hold over certain parts of the globe, restoring the Earth's climate. They have accomplished the seemingly impossible and Earth-saving feat, allowing for a chance for change and a lesson to those who listen.

EPILOGUE

Mr. Davenport walks past his crew up to the sanctuary. He leans his head in first, not wanting to disturb whoever may be inside. However, he almost immediately decides to enter. His eyes fixed on Sara in her elegant silk robes. The robes resemble the one Angelina had to bear while in the Goddess's mental confinement. However, these appear to have Sara's spin upon them. Ocean blue intertwined into the green material.

"You look official," Mr. Davenport states.

"Don't mock."

He smiles, knowing neither one believes this to be so. Neither one ever was direct with the other, although they held a form of respect. Yet, Davenport would not given Sara's new role. He was more than glad she was the one who took the mantle, and Angelina stepped away after over a thousand years under the Goddess's control. It has led the globe into a new era of calamity.

"I'd love to see what you've done with the place."

"Of course, Scott." Sara steps forward, knowing that he follows wherever she goes. They go through the intertwined vines, the opening of the sanctuary. Mr. Davenport's eyes linger on where the tents we set up.

He found it strange on the way in that they were no longer there. Although, he knows that Sara will elude him to this in the coming moments. She is not for prolonged mysteries as the Goddess before she was. It is another reason why Mr. Davenport appreciates Sara's rein. She has a more direct approach.

"They've moved into the Temple…. They've worshipped the walls since Angelina and I— Since we settled things," Sara explains. "I think they'll be back soon. It's what Charles and Angelina say anyway."

"Sounds right," Davenport agrees. "Why worship walls when you worship the woman that helped guide the world into a better life." Sara bashfully smiles, not thinking much of her contribution. Though, she continues to lead Mr. Davenport through the campsite. Further out to where Angelina showed Sara her prophesied future, the Temple, to where the people have gathered.

"They're this way," she states. "I think you'll like the progress we've made…. It looks a lot better, a lot like before. I think anyway. It's just a little tiring. I mean, the Temple, people on top of my new gig."

Mr. Davenport pauses, knowing Sara is going through changes, emotional and mental growth, having to hold the balance of the earth and those living on it. It is a lot of responsibility for one person to have. Luckily, Sara has the aid of Angelina, Charles, and all living within their near vicinity.

"Yes, well, I imagine trying to restore a temple would do that to you."

"True." Although he has much to say regarding her contributions and what is yet to come, she and Mr. Davenport continue on the path without another word. Though he still appears conscious, watching his step. Almost certain of what will happen, Sara's eyes occasionally shift to his feet, fearing the wild plants stretching across the path.

Sara has been subject to many surprises since her unorthodox inauguration. Snakes in the sanctuary and birds enclosing a section of forestation. Before what Sara had experienced alongside Angelina, she would have been frightened. However, Sara now expects these experiences with life in the rainforest and is somehow connected to them like the planet.

Before Mr. Davenport can notice, he trips over a fading piece of tile from the Temple. They are closing in on the people and their setup outside the ruins. Luckily, Sara was prepared for such a misstep and reached her hand out to prevent his fall. After a short moment to collect himself, Mr. Davenport looks at Sara with something she does not recognize resting behind his eyes.

"Thank you."

Rather than reply, Sara smiles at him as she cannot acknowledge what is coming her way. With Mr. Davenport, Sara knows more about him than she had thought. It was more a sense from him. It was familiar as if she had already known him. Despite her initial distrust in him based on Charles and the Goddess's words, Sara had found herself somewhat comfortable in his presence.

Although now she is aware of why everything in her life led her to the worldwide disasters and her connections to what seems to be everything, Sara has learned everything already has their place in her memory and instinct. She is also sure Mr. Davenport has learned of this too. The worshipers he had taken in after the ground-shaking and disorienting that had taken place would have filled him in. Fortunately, it did not take long for the followers to return to their place and the Temple.

Yet, this does not change Mr. Davenport's interest in all transpiring here, his connection to Sara, and the land they stand on. As if knowing what is on Sara's mind, Davenport returns his gaze. However, it is not the friendly smile and awkward stance Sara has become accustomed to. He is concerned, and his shoulders move like something rests on them.

"You'll do great," Davenport states. "I've heard about the tiles.... and everything you've been seeing. It's a lot."

"How would you deal with it? Being told what you will accomplish and how it will all end?" Though he intends to help Sara in this manner, he knows there is not much he can do. Especially when he does not know the burden of such a high power as Sara now does. Nor does he need to endure the truth of the coming future.

"I don't know," Mr. Davenport replies. "I was always the kind of guy that prefers to make it up as he goes along."

"There's so much more to do."

A soft smile stretches across his mug, knowing she will face many challenges as she continues to work for harmonization. "Then you'll do what is needed. Prophesied or not, you'll make the right decision."

"How are you so sure?" Sara asks.

Mr. Davenport steps forward, walking to the center of the camp. He lifts his arms, gesturing to those around him. Sara bows her head, trying to hide the rush of blood. However, she knows that it is too late. Mr. Davenport saw her embarrassment. Although, neither one says anything. They only wait a moment before Sara walks over to Mr. Davenport.

"You have a lot of faith in me."

"We all do," Davenport says. "Now... I'm still waiting to see how far you've come with the Temple."

Sara continues to walk with Mr. Davenport before he notices the wall stretching along the forestation. Unlike before, he is more cautious and mindful of debris under his feet. Luckily, there is not much on the ground anymore. The followers must have been clearing them away.

Yet, Mr. Davenport does not focus too much on the ground under his feet. The wall Davenport noted has various tiles. However, they are not as worn down as he expected. They appear refurbished. Perhaps it is what the followers have lost themselves in. They want to know what else will take place, to read what has already transpired and what they believe is taking place.

"So.... These are the tiles?"

"That's them," Sara confirms.

Mr. Davenport nods. He cannot say anything of use or particularly fitting. There was only so much he could have said before on secondhand information, but now, he sees why Sara is put off and reluctant. Not only does this wall symbolize what has happened for millennia, it details her past and what appears to be the end of the world. She will reign with the title of Mother Nature until the earth's ultimate death.

"This is...." Mr. Davenport trails off. "Well, they did make your hair look amazing." Sara scoffs with her eyes trained on Davenport. He soon returns her gaze, hoping she will understand what is underlying.

"It's a lot of responsibility."

Mr. Davenport stays silent, staring at the tiles before him. He searches for something to say. However, there is not much he can do to ease her worries and fate. She has caught him at a loss for words. Davenport takes a step back and looks into Sara's eyes. For a moment, neither one moves. They only stare at each other. Yet, Davenport is the first to break this uneasy and tense trance they share.

"You'll be the calm in the storm. You'll help settle things and make things easier."

"And what will be left for me? Once this is over, I'll watch as the world and everyone I've been responsible for dies," Sara expresses.

Davenport becomes silent again as if to seriously consider what Sara had to say, to think of a way to comfort her. Yet, he knows there is no use when she faces something as unfair as this.

"Well, there's not much to say. Can you even do anything about the sun burning out? Everything eventually comes to an end. It's what you do in the face of that and what you do to make things the best they can before it does," Mr. Davenport enlightens. "And that's you, Sara.... You'll be the one to help guide and lead everyone into a better now, to enjoy what we have before things end."

Tears cloud Sara's eyes. She redirects her attention to those gathered further down, reading the permanent transcript. "You'll help them," Davenport stresses.

Sara eventually retrains her eyes to look at Mr. Davenport again. However, there appears to be something else in her expression now, giving Mr. Davenport a small hope that he has reached her. "Thank you."

They stare at each other again, although now Sara and Davenport have a sense of peace and acceptance that neither of them had before their discussion and unfortunate circumstances.

END.